The Black Cat and the Ghoul

by Edgar Allan Poe
and Keith Gouveia

Also by Edgar Allan Poe

(In Life)

Tamerlane and Other Poems
Al Aaraaf, Tamerlane and Minor Poems
Poems
Tales of the Grotesque and Arabesque
The Prose Romances of Edgar A. Poe
Tales
The Raven and Other Poems

(After Death)

The Fall of the House of Usher
Famous Tales of Mystery and Horror
Edgar Allan Poe: Poetry and Tales
Edgar Allan Poe's Tales of Mystery and Madness
Edgar Allan Poe's Complete Poetical Works
Great Short Works of Edgar Allan Poe
Great Tales and Poems of Edgar Allan Poe
The Portable Edgar Allan Poe
The Complete Works of Edgar Allan Poe
Edgar Allan Poe's Tales of Death and Dementia
The Murders in the Rue Morgue
The Narrative of Arthur Gordon Pym of Nantucket

Also by Keith Gouveia

(In Life)

The Eternal Battle
Dream Demon
Killing Faith
The Evil Men Do
Children of the Dragon
A Storm To Remember
Grave Cravings (with Garrett Peck)
The Goblin Princess
Devil's Playground (with A.P. Fuchs)
On Hell's Wings (with A.P. Fuchs)
Bits of the Dead (editor)
Death Puppet: Revolt of the Dead
Animal Behavior and Other Tales of Lycanthropy
Behind the Stained Glass
The Snuff Syndicate
The Screaming Field

Published 2014 by Beating Windward Press LLC

For contact information, please visit:
www.BeatingWindward.com

Second Edition
ISBN: 978-1-940761-06-0

TABLE OF CONTENTS

INTRODUCTION

When I look back at the life of Edgar Allan Poe it's easy to see where the darkness that permeates his writing stemmed from. Edgar Poe—born January 19, 1809, and dying October 7, 1849—suffered many tragedies within those scant forty years. Abandoned by his father and facing his mother's untimely death shortly thereafter, he was taken in by John and Frances Allan who never saw fit to legally adopt him. He enrolled in the University of Virginia, but was forced to drop out due to financial concerns. Unable to support himself, he enlisted in the army only to fail—purposefully, I might add—as an officer's cadet; and he lost his beloved wife, Virginia Clemm, to tuberculosis after a twelve-year romance. All these hardships shaped and defined the man's writing, poetry and prose, that, to this day, is cherished by countless readers. Considered the inventor of the detective fiction genre and credited with the emerging genre of science fiction, Poe's tales and poems have withstood the test of time and prove poignant even today.

Unfortunately, though, for Poe, his work never received the accolades it enjoys these days while he was alive. During his life he was notable mainly as a literary critic. His first collection of poetry was published under the byline "a Bostonian"; his collection *Tales of the Grotesque and Arabesque* received mixed reviews; and though "The Raven" made him a household name, he earned a paltry nine dollars for its publication.

Still, the man persevered, determined to make a living at what he loved doing and had it been a different time, a different place, surely he would have seen great success. One thing's for sure: had he given up, the world would be a duller place.

I'd hate to think where I would be and what kind of a man I'd see staring back in the mirror if it weren't for the writings of Poe. The darkness found in his words connected to the darkness I tried so hard to bury and hide from the world in my youth. His words reminded me I wasn't alone and that there was an outlet for it—and no, I'm not talking about alcohol, but writing.

In my earlier school years I was too cool to be caught reading, dismissed homework assignments, and barely scraped by on my test scores. That all changed after an eighth grade field trip to the Providence Performing Arts Center to see a trio of plays based on short works of fiction. The teacher asked us to read the stories we were to bear witness to so we could notice the subtle, necessary changes made to the text for the translation from paper to stage. In the days that led up to that class trip my attitude was pretty much the same as all the other boys in my class. Plays? Bleh! Poetry? That's for girls.

Movies is where it's at.

I didn't read the stories beforehand and had it not been mandatory and forced upon me, I probably never would have gone to the Arts Center, and I would have missed out on a truly wonderful experience. I have to say the Providence Performing Arts Center is a grand building and I remember being awestruck as we walked its halls before being ushered to our seats. When the red velvet curtain finally went up, I watched, spellbound, as the actors and actresses acted out "The Raven," "The Monkey's Paw," and, finally, "The Tell-Tale Heart." The best was absolutely saved for last and though, when it was said and done, most of the boys still snubbed their noses, I was forever changed.

During the bus ride home I couldn't stop thinking about Poe and where I had read that name before; then it dawned on me, and I couldn't wait to get home. I can't remember if it was the week before the field trip or earlier, but we were given order forms for a book drive and one of the books in the catalogue just happened to be a small paperback collection of Poe tales: *Famous Tales of Mystery and Horror*—which after twenty-plus years still sits proudly on my bookshelf beside *The Complete Works of Edgar Allan Poe*. As an adult, I can see those tales in that little paperback were selected for a younger audience, but at the time, I had to have it. I remembered the book from the catalogue solely for its cover of a skull wearing a ballroom mask and not for the author's name, which I am ashamed of. If only I had done my homework as asked, Poe would have entered my life earlier.

When that book finally arrived, I devoured every word and sought more. After reading all of his short stories, I swallowed my pride and read some of his poetry. Suddenly, poetry didn't seem girly or un-cool to me, and when I tried to emulate Poe's poems, I had a deeper understanding of poetry's intricate qualities. Though I have a greater appreciation for the aesthetic art and try my hand at it occasionally, I have yet to master the form. I have resolved myself to the fact I lack rhythm; I simply write them for fun or as exercises to get the creative juices flowing.

Eventually I broke away from the other kids who disagreed with my reading tastes, and after reading all of Poe's works, I branched out into novels with similar themes. Slowly, but surely, my grades improved. I actually made the honor roll in the last quarter of eighth grade, earning myself an elusive Morton M—a patch that I still have to this day. Upon entering high school, I took my studies seriously—most of the time, anyway. I still slacked on occasion. After all, it's what teenagers do.

For me, the book you are holding in your hands or on your eReader is more than a gimmick, it's a way for me to say thank you to Edgar, and to keep his spirit alive and well in the hearts of future readers. When I was approached by Coscom Entertainment to do a literary mash-up, I turned it down. It didn't feel right for me, especially considering how many original ideas I have of my own. But A.P. Fuchs was persistent and eventually wore me down—after almost a year—when he asked if I'd be interested in doing something with Edgar Allan

Poe, my immediate reaction was *blasphemy*. But I knew if I didn't do it, someone else would and I wasn't about to let just anyone hack 'n' slash my beloved treasures. Before responding to his email, *Poe's Lighthouse* edited by Christopher Conlon and published by Cemetery Dance Publications came to mind. After Poe's death, an untitled story fragment was found in his papers. Conlon invited twenty-three authors to finish the tale. Each one is unique in tone and theme, and though well worth the read, the collection is pricey, but the idea was solid. And sadly, no, I was not one of the invited. And now thanks to Beating Windward Press, the book is getting a second chance.

"The Black Cat" was, for me, the one piece of Poe's that felt unfinished. In "The Black Cat" our narrator is an unnamed man, and the story's precise locale is also unknown. It dawned on me to use this opportunity to answer all the nagging questions the story left me with. It is the opening to my novella, in its original text, and used as a springboard. Whether or not I took the story in a natural direction, one worthy of Poe, is up to you, the reader. Though I love Poe's work, my continuation of his story is written in my voice with selective words Poe would have used. This was done with younger readers in mind, to hopefully not bore or bog them down with the use of old language. Considering all of Poe's work is short, save for *The Narrative of Arthur Gordon Pym of Nantucket*—Poe's only novel—I feel taken in small doses, the old language adds to the allure, and should not hamper anyone's enjoyment of the works. However, I have seen many shy away from his work because of it, which is a shame, really.

Included with this novella is my poem "Cemetery," inspired by the novella I wrote and one of my favorite Poe poems, "The City in the Sea." It was difficult to choose just one of Poe's poems to include, but it is the one that best represents the overall theme of this book. If you enjoy it, I recommend searching for "Alone," "Annabel Lee," and "Spirits of the Dead," all favorites of mine and all free to read online. Also, of course, Poe's "The Tell-Tale Heart" just because of how special it is to me. Also included, my short story homage to one of horror's finest masters, "Broken" which was originally published in *Dreaded Pall*, 2007.

I hope in reading this, my enthusiasm for Poe's work shines through and rubs off on you.

Until next time, nevermore.

Cemetery
by
Keith Gouveia

There is a place, so dark and cruel
Where shadows dance and lurk and rule
Where dead men reside and lovers dwell
And Insects cause decay's excel

Once confined in this dreary place
There are two paths that one may grace
Resting in glory of Heaven's sacred keep
Or screaming in fire of Hell's black deep

The living dare not venture through
While in the earth we silently brood
Is it fear or shame keeping them away?
I wonder, does their guilt heavily weigh?

No more wanderers through these rows
We do not ask for much, why oppose?
Just one visit, or have you forgotten?
Living life while our bodies rotten

No one sees the spirits' restlessness
But not all the residents are motionless
I have discarded death's loathsome throes
So I may appease their lonely woes

At night I visit the graves one-by-one
And return to my crypt at the rising sun
I hunger, over living flesh I drool
You can call me undead, zombie, or ghoul

The City in the Sea
by
Edgar Allan Poe

Lo! Death has reared himself a throne
In a strange city lying alone
Far down within the dim West,
Where the good and the bad and the worst and the best
Have gone to their eternal rest.
There shrines and palaces and towers
(Time-eaten towers that tremble not!)
Resemble nothing that is ours.
Around, by lifting winds forgot,
Resignedly beneath the sky
The melancholy waters lie.

No rays from the holy heaven come down
On the long night-time of that town;
But light from out the lurid sea

Streams up the turrets silently—
Gleams up the pinnacles far and free—
Up domes- up spires- up kingly halls—
Up fanes- up Babylon-like walls—
Up shadowy long-forgotten bowers
Of sculptured ivy and stone flowers—
Up many and many a marvellous shrine
Whose wreathed friezes intertwine
The viol, the violet, and the vine.
Resignedly beneath the sky
The melancholy waters lie.
So blend the turrets and shadows there
That all seem pendulous in air,
While from a proud tower in the town
Death looks gigantically down.

There open fanes and gaping graves
Yawn level with the luminous waves;
But not the riches there that lie
In each idol's diamond eye—
Not the gaily-jewelled dead
Tempt the waters from their bed;
For no ripples curl, alas!
Along that wilderness of glass—
No swellings tell that winds may be
Upon some far-off happier sea—
No heavings hint that winds have been
On seas less hideously serene.

But lo, a stir is in the air!
The wave- there is a movement there!
As if the towers had thrust aside,
In slightly sinking, the dull tide—
As if their tops had feebly given
A void within the filmy Heaven.
The waves have now a redder glow—
The hours are breathing faint and low—
And when, amid no earthly moans,
Down, down that town shall settle hence,
Hell, rising from a thousand thrones,
Shall do it reverence.

The Black Cat And The Ghoul

CHAPTER ONE

For the most wild, yet most homely narrative which I am about to pen, I neither expect nor solicit belief. Mad indeed would I be to expect it, in a case where my very senses reject their own evidence. Yet, mad am I not—and very surely do I not dream. But to-morrow I die, and to-day I would unburthen my soul. My immediate purpose is to place before the world, plainly, succinctly, and without comment, a series of mere household events. In their consequences, these events have terrified—have tortured—have destroyed me. Yet I will not attempt to expound them. To me, they have presented little but Horror—to many they will seem less terrible than baroques. Hereafter, perhaps, some intellect may be found which will reduce my phantasm to the common-place—some intellect more calm, more logical, and far less excitable than my own, which will perceive, in the circumstances I detail with awe, nothing more than an ordinary succession of very natural causes and effects.

From my infancy I was noted for the docility and humanity of my disposition. My tenderness of heart was even so conspicuous as to make me the jest of my companions. I was especially fond of animals, and was indulged by my parents with a great variety of pets. With these I spent most of my time, and never was so happy as when feeding and caressing them. This peculiarity of character grew with my growth, and, in my manhood, I derived from it one of my principal sources of pleasure. To those who have cherished an affection for a faithful and sagacious dog, I need hardly be at the trouble of explaining the nature or the intensity of the gratification thus derivable. There is something in the unselfish and self-sacrificing love of a brute, which goes directly to the heart of him who has had frequent occasion to test the paltry friendship and gossamer fidelity of mere Man.

I married early, and was happy to find in my wife a disposition not uncongenial with my own. Observing my partiality for domestic pets, she lost no opportunity of procuring those of the most agreeable kind. We had birds, gold-fish, a fine dog, rabbits, a small monkey, and a cat.

This latter was a remarkably large and beautiful animal, entirely black, and sagacious to an astonishing degree. In speaking of his intelligence, my wife, who at heart was not a little tinctured with superstition, made frequent allusion to the ancient popular notion, which regarded all black cats as witches in disguise. Not that she was ever *serious* upon this point—and I mention the matter at all for no better reason than that it happens, just now, to be remembered.

Pluto—this was the cat's name—was my favorite pet and playmate. I alone fed him, and he attended me wherever I went about the house. It was even with difficulty that I could prevent him from following me through the streets.

Our friendship lasted, in this manner, for several years, during which my general temperament and character—through the instrumentality of the Fiend Intemperance—had (I blush to confess it) experienced a radical alteration for the worse. I grew, day by day, more moody, more irritable, more regardless of the feelings of others. I suffered myself to use intemperate language to my wife. At length, I even offered her personal violence. My pets, of course, were made to feel the change in my disposition. I not only neglected, but ill-used them. For Pluto, however, I still retained sufficient regard to restrain me from maltreating him, as I made no scruple of maltreating the rabbits, the monkey, or even the dog, when by accident, or through affection, they came in my way. But my disease grew upon me—for what disease is like Alcohol!—and at length even Pluto, who was now becoming old, and consequently somewhat peevish—even Pluto began to experience the effects of my ill temper.

One night, returning home, much intoxicated, from one of my haunts about town, I fancied that the cat avoided my presence. I seized him; when, in his fright at my violence, he inflicted a slight wound upon my hand with his teeth. The fury of a demon instantly possessed me. I knew myself no longer.

My original soul seemed, at once, to take its flight from my body; and a more than fiendish malevolence, gin-nurtured, thrilled every fiber of my frame. I took from my waistcoat-pocket a pen-knife, opened it, grasped the poor beast by the throat, and deliberately cut one of its eyes from the socket! I blush, I burn, I shudder, while I pen the damnable atrocity.

When reason returned with the morning—when I had slept off the fumes of the night's debauch—I experienced a sentiment half of horror, half of remorse, for the crime of which I had been guilty; but it was, at best, a feeble and equivocal feeling, and the soul remained untouched. I again plunged into excess, and soon drowned in wine all memory of the deed.

In the meantime the cat slowly recovered. The socket of the lost eye presented, it is true, a frightful appearance, but he no longer appeared to suffer any pain. He went about the house as usual, but, as might be expected, fled in extreme terror at my approach. I had so much of my old heart left, as to be at first grieved by this evident dislike on the part of a creature which had once so loved me. But this feeling soon gave place to irritation. And then came, as if to my final and irrevocable overthrow, the spirit of PERVERSENESS. Of this spirit philosophy takes no account. Yet I am not more sure that my soul lives, than I am that perverseness is one of the primitive impulses of the human heart—one of the indivisible primary faculties, or sentiments, which give direction to the character of Man. Who has not, a hundred times, found himself committing a vile or a silly action, for no other reason than because he knows he should *not*? Have we not a perpetual inclination, in the teeth of our best judgment, to violate that which is Law, merely because we understand it to be such? This spirit of perverseness, I say, came to my final overthrow. It was this unfathomable longing of the soul to vex itself—to offer violence to its own nature—to do wrong for the wrong's sake only—that urged me to continue and finally to consummate the injury I had inflicted upon the unoffending brute. One morning, in cool blood, I slipped a noose about its neck and hung it to the limb of a tree; hung it with the tears streaming from my eyes, and with the bitterest remorse at my heart; hung it *because* I knew that it had loved me, and because I felt it had given me no reason of offence; hung it *because* I knew that in so doing I was committing a sin—a deadly sin that would so jeopardize my immortal soul as to place it— if such a thing were possible—even beyond the reach of the infinite mercy of the Most Merciful and Most Terrible God.

On the night of the day on which this cruel deed was done, I was aroused from sleep by the cry of fire. The curtains of my bed were in flames. The whole house was blazing. It was with great difficulty that my wife, a servant, and myself, made our escape from the conflagration. The destruction was complete. My entire worldly wealth was swallowed up, and I resigned myself thenceforward to despair.

I am above the weakness of seeking to establish a sequence of cause and effect, between the disaster and the atrocity. But I am detailing a chain of facts—and wish not to leave even a possible link imperfect. On the day succeeding the fire, I visited the ruins. The walls, with one exception, had fallen in. This exception was found in a compartment wall, not very thick, which stood about the middle of the house, and against which had rested the head of my bed. The plastering had here, in great measure, resisted the action of the fire—a fact which I attributed to its having been recently spread. About this wall a dense crowd were collected, and many persons seemed to be examining a particular portion of it with very minute and eager attention. The words "strange!" "singular!" and other similar expressions, excited my curiosity. I approached and saw, as if graven in *bas relief* upon the white surface, the figure of a gigantic *cat*. The impression was given with an accuracy truly marvelous. There was a rope about the animal's neck.

When I first beheld this apparition—for I could scarcely regard it as less—my wonder and my terror were extreme. But at length reflection came to my aid. The cat, I remembered, had been hung in a garden adjacent to the house. Upon the alarm of fire, this garden had been immediately filled by the crowd—by some one of whom the animal must have been cut from the tree and thrown, through an open window, into my chamber. This had probably been done with the view of arousing me from sleep. The falling of other walls had compressed the victim of my cruelty into the substance of the freshly-spread plaster; the lime of which, with the flames, and the ammonia from the carcass, had then accomplished the portraiture as I saw it.

Although I thus readily accounted to my reason, if not altogether to my conscience, for the startling fact just detailed, it did not the less fail to make a deep impression upon my fancy. For months I could not rid myself of the phantasm of the cat; and, during this period, there came back into my spirit a half-sentiment that seemed, but was not, remorse. I went so far as to regret the loss of the animal, and to look about me, among the vile haunts which I now habitually frequented, for another pet of the same species, and of somewhat similar appearance, with which to supply its place.

One night as I sat, half stupefied, in a den of more than infamy, my attention was suddenly drawn to some black object, reposing upon the head of one of the immense hogsheads of Gin, or of Rum, which constituted the chief furniture of the apartment. I had been looking steadily at the top of this hogshead for some minutes, and what now caused me surprise was the fact that I had not sooner perceived the object thereupon. I approached it, and touched it with my hand. It was a black cat—a very large one—fully as large as Pluto, and closely resembling him in every respect but one. Pluto had not a white hair upon any portion of his body; but this cat had a large, although indefinite splotch of white, covering nearly the whole region of the breast.

Upon my touching him, he immediately arose, purred loudly, rubbed against my hand, and appeared delighted with my notice. This, then, was the very creature of which I was in search. I at once offered to purchase it of the landlord; but this person made no claim to it—knew nothing of it—had never seen it before.

I continued my caresses, and, when I prepared to go home, the animal evinced a disposition to accompany me. I permitted it to do so; occasionally stooping and patting it as I proceeded. When it reached the house it domesticated itself at once, and became immediately a great favorite with my wife.

For my own part, I soon found a dislike to it arising within me. This was just the reverse of what I had anticipated; but—I know not how or why it was—its evident fondness for myself rather disgusted and annoyed. By slow degrees, these feelings of disgust and annoyance rose into the bitterness of hatred. I avoided the creature; a certain sense of shame, and the remembrance of my former deed of cruelty, preventing me from physically abusing it. I did not, for some weeks, strike, or otherwise violently ill use it; but gradually—very gradually—I came to look upon it with unutterable loathing, and to flee silently from its odious presence, as from the breath of a pestilence.

What added, no doubt, to my hatred of the beast, was the discovery, on the morning after I brought it home, that, like Pluto, it also had been deprived of one of its eyes. This circumstance, however, only endeared it to my wife, who, as I have already said, possessed, in a high degree, that humanity of feeling which had once been my distinguishing trait, and the source of many of my simplest and purest pleasures.

With my aversion to this cat, however, its partiality for myself seemed to increase. It followed my footsteps with a pertinacity which it would be difficult to make the reader comprehend. Whenever I sat, it would crouch beneath my chair, or spring upon my knees, covering me with its loathsome caresses. If I arose to walk it would get between my feet and thus nearly throw me down, or, fastening its long and sharp claws in my dress, clamber, in this manner, to my breast. At such times, although I longed to destroy it with a blow, I was yet withheld from so doing, partly by a memory of my former crime, but chiefly—let me confess it at once—by absolute *dread* of the beast.

This dread was not exactly a dread of physical evil—and yet I should be at a loss how otherwise to define it. I am almost ashamed to own—yes, even in this felon's cell, I am almost ashamed to own—that the terror and horror with which the animal inspired me, had been heightened by one of the merest chimeras it would be possible to conceive. My wife had called my attention, more than once, to the character of the mark of white hair, of which I have spoken, and which constituted the sole visible difference between the strange beast and the one I had destroyed. The reader will remember that this mark, although large, had been originally very indefinite; but, by slow degrees—degrees nearly imperceptible, and which for a long time my Reason struggled to reject as fanciful—it had, at length, assumed a rigorous distinctness of an outline. It was now the representation of an object that I shudder to name— and for this, above all, I loathed, and dreaded, and would have rid myself of the monster had I dared—it was now, I say, the image of a hideous—of a ghastly thing—of the GALLOWS! —oh, mournful and terrible engine of Horror and of Crime— of Agony and of Death!

And now was I indeed wretched beyond the wretchedness of mere Humanity. And *a brute beast*—whose fellow I had contemptuously destroyed—*a brute beast* to work out for me— for me a man, fashioned in the image of the High God—so much of insufferable wo! Alas! Neither by day nor by night knew I the blessing of Rest any more! During the former the creature left me no moment alone; and, in the latter, I started, hourly, from dreams of unutterable fear, to find the hot breath of the thing upon my face, and its vast weight—an incarnate Night-Mare that I had no power to shake off—incumbent eternally upon my heart!

Beneath the pressure of torments such as these, the feeble remnant of the good within me succumbed. Evil thoughts became my sole intimates—the darkest and most evil of thoughts. The moodiness of my usual temper increased to hatred of all things and of all mankind; while, from the sudden, frequent, and ungovernable outbursts of a fury to which I now blindly abandoned myself, my uncomplaining wife, alas! was the most usual and the most patient of sufferers.

One day she accompanied me, upon some household errand, into the cellar of the old building which our poverty compelled us to inhabit. The cat followed me down the steep stairs, and, nearly throwing me headlong, exasperated me to madness. Uplifting an axe, and forgetting, in my wrath, the childish dread which had hitherto stayed my hand, I aimed a blow at the animal which, of course, would have proved instantly fatal had it descended as I wished. But this blow was arrested by the hand of my wife. Goaded, by the interference, into a rage more than demoniacal, I withdrew my arm from her grasp and buried the axe in her brain. She fell dead upon the spot, without a groan.

This hideous murder accomplished, I set myself forthwith, and with entire deliberation, to the task of concealing the body. I knew that I could not remove it from the house, either by day or by night, without the risk of being observed by the neighbors. Many projects entered my mind. At one period I thought of cutting the corpse into minute fragments, and destroying them by fire. At another, I resolved to dig a grave for it in the floor of the cellar. Again, I deliberated about casting it in the well in the yard—about packing it in a box, as if merchandize, with the usual arrangements, and so getting a porter to take it from the house. Finally I hit upon what I considered a far better expedient than either of these. I determined to wall it up in the cellar—as the monks of the middle ages are recorded to have walled up their victims.

For a purpose such as this the cellar was well adapted. Its walls were loosely constructed, and had lately been plastered throughout with a rough plaster, which the dampness of the atmosphere had prevented from hardening. Moreover, in one of the walls was a projection, caused by a false chimney, or fireplace, that had been filled up, and made to resemble the rest of the cellar. I made no doubt that I could readily displace the bricks at this point, insert the corpse, and wall the whole up as before, so that no eye could detect anything suspicious.

And in this calculation I was not deceived. By means of a crow-bar I easily dislodged the bricks, and, having carefully deposited the body against the inner wall, I propped it in that position, while, with little trouble, I re-laid the whole structure as it originally stood. Having procured mortar, sand, and hair, with every possible precaution, I prepared a plaster which could not be distinguished from the old, and with this I very carefully went over the new brick-work. When I had finished, I felt satisfied that all was right. The wall did not present the slightest appearance of having been disturbed. The rubbish on the floor was picked up with the minutest care. I looked around triumphantly, and said to myself—"Here at least, then, my labor has not been in vain."

My next step was to look for the beast which had been the cause of so much wretchedness; for I had, at length, firmly resolved to put it to death. Had I been able to meet with it, at the moment, there could have been no doubt of its fate; but it appeared that the crafty animal had been alarmed at the violence of my previous anger, and forbore to present itself in my present mood. It is impossible to describe, or to imagine, the deep, the blissful sense of relief which the absence of the detested creature occasioned in my bosom. It did not make its appearance during the night—and thus for one night at least, since its introduction into the house, I soundly and tranquilly slept; aye, slept even with the burden of murder upon my soul!

The second and the third day passed, and still my tormentor came not. Once again I breathed as a freeman. The monster, in terror, had fled the premises forever! I should behold it no more! My happiness was supreme! The guilt of my dark deed disturbed me but little. Some few inquiries had been made, but these had been readily answered. Even a search had been instituted—but of course nothing was to be discovered. I looked upon my future felicity as secured.

Upon the fourth day of the assassination, a party of the police came, very unexpectedly, into the house, and proceeded again to make rigorous investigation of the premises. Secure, however, in the inscrutability of my place of concealment, I felt no embarrassment whatever. The officers bade me accompany them in their search. They left no nook or corner unexplored. At length, for the third or fourth time, they descended into the cellar. I quivered not in a muscle. My heart beat calmly as that of one who slumbers in innocence. I walked the cellar from end to end. I folded my arms upon my bosom, and roamed easily to and fro. The police were thoroughly satisfied and prepared to depart. The glee at my heart was too strong to be restrained. I burned to say if but one word, by way of triumph, and to render doubly sure their assurance of my guiltlessness.

"Gentlemen," I said at last, as the party ascended the steps, "I delight to have allayed your suspicions. I wish you all health, and a little more courtesy. By the bye, gentlemen, this—this is a very well constructed house." (In the rabid desire to say something easily, I scarcely knew what I uttered at all.) — "I may say an *excellently* well constructed house. These walls—are you going, gentlemen?—these walls are solidly put together;" and here, through the mere phrenzy of bravado, I rapped heavily, with a cane which I held in my hand, upon that very portion of the brick-work behind which stood the corpse of the wife of my bosom.

But may God shield and deliver me from the fangs of the Arch-Fiend! No sooner had the reverberation of my blows sunk into silence, than I was answered by a voice from within the tomb! —by a cry, at first muffled and broken, like the sobbing of a child, and then quickly swelling into one long, loud, and continuous scream, utterly anomalous and inhuman—a howl—a wailing shriek, half of horror and half of triumph, such as might have arisen only out of Hell, conjointly from the throats of the damned in their agony, and of the demons that exult in the damnation.

Of my own thoughts it is folly to speak. Swooning, I staggered to the opposite wall. For one instant the party upon the stairs remained motionless, through extremity of terror and of awe. In the next, a dozen stout arms were toiling at the wall. It fell bodily. The corpse, already greatly decayed and clotted with gore, stood erect before the eyes of the spectators. Upon its head, with red extended mouth and solitary eye of fire, sat the hideous beast whose craft had seduced me into murder, and whose informing voice had consigned me to the hangman. I had walled the monster up within the tomb!

CHAPTER TWO

"At it again I see, eh, John?"

John breathed heavily through his nose, tired of the jailer's constant mockery. "One last chance," he finally said as he deposited his quill, then scooped up the handwritten pages.

"You using them pretty words of yours? Showing off that there education?"

John stuffed the pages into a large envelope and said, "I take it you've read one of my manuscripts, then?"

The jailer looked away, confirming John's suspicion.

"As long as it reached its destination, I see no harm. Would you be so kind as to mail this for me as well? Think of it as a dying man's last request." He licked the envelope's edge and sealed it, then extended his arm to pass the envelope between the bars of his cell to the wretch of a man.

The jailer took the envelope and peered at its face. "The *Saturday Evening Post*, huh? Poor choice. It's a respectable paper and I for one doubt they'll be interested in the ravings of a lunatic."

If only the court had seen it that way, perhaps I'd be in finer accommodations. But I wonder . . . how many will think me mad once they've read my manuscript? "Humor me."

The jailer smiled a toothy grin, exposing blackened gums and yellowed teeth. He nodded and walked away.

When he started writing his tale of woe and sending it out to various magazines and papers, it was in the hopes of amassing sympathy for his plight—to escape the hangman's noose. But now, with death looming over him, it seemed to be the only way to carry on his family name. With no children to call his own, the Mohr name would be purged from the annals of history.

John Mohr stood from his writing table and walked over toward the barred window of his cell. His gaze fixated on the gallows. The weathered wood and rope looked ominous in the moonlight. He swallowed hard as he pictured his swaying body in the autumn wind, dangling below the platform from the noose.

I hope my head stays upon my shoulders, he thought. He had heard on numerous occasions of men being decapitated during the process. *Best not to think about it. It's not like my head will do me any good where I'm going anyway.* He turned away and looked to the four walls he had called home for the past six months. *At least I shall be free of this cage once more.*

He closed his eyes and pictured the twelve faces that had sent him to this dreary place. They had looked upon him with such disdain, and the foreman looked as though he took too much pleasure out of reading the jurors' verdict of "guilty." John could still see that sickening smirk and the man's narrowed eyes as he spoke. They acted as if he was the first man in history to kill his spouse.

I'd love to be given the chance to choke the life out of each one of them and spit on their rotting carcasses, he thought.

"Look what we found wandering outside," said the jailer as he returned.

John felt his eyes go wide and a hard lump form in his throat. Nestled in the jailer's arms, the one-eyed cat purred as he stroked its black fur. It sat up, revealing the white patch of fur on its breast. In that blotch John Mohr saw his death. The jailer's keys jingled as he unlocked the cell door.

"What are you doing? Stay back!"

The sheer sight of the animal stirred his emotions: fear, regret, hatred, and betrayal all bubbled to the surface. "Keep that feral beast away from me," he said, eyeing the cause of his madness.

"I figure you could use some company for your last night." The guard opened the door, bent forward, and released the cat into the cell. "No man should be alone at such a dark time." He closed the door and the cat stepped toward him.

John jumped on his cot and scooted backward until his back hit the wall. The cat leapt onto the other end of the cot and sat, then began the tedious task of grooming itself.

It's mocking me, he thought, for he knew the beast to be a cold, calculating monstrosity born from the fires of Hell.

"Enjoy your last moments together," said the jailer as he walked away.

"Don't leave me alone with it," he said, but his plea fell upon deaf ears.

He looked deep into the feline's eye, trying to keep the barren void out of his peripheral vision, and tried to shoo the beast away with the power of influence from his mind, but the damnable beast remained perched and stared back at him.

Wretched vermin has already signed my death warrant. What more can it do to me?

CHAPTER THREE

Minutes passed as if they were hours. The snoring from the guard down the hall wafted into his cell and John longed to sleep—to forget. But how could anyone sleep with such an evil glare staring back at them? Soon he would sleep eternally, but not before purging this earth of this vile creature.

Frustrated, and with nothing left to lose, he reached out and grabbed the black cat around the neck. He had expected it to claw or bite him, like it had during their last struggle, but instead it lovingly purred, shocking him even further. The purring increased an octave as the pressure around its throat tightened.

"Die! And this time, stay dead!"

A fire ignited in the wasteland of the cat's eye. Embers danced around its head and John's hands retreated. The walls of the cell around him caught fire; the brickwork and iron bars melted away to reveal a vast room. In the center, a fountain of molten lava spewed forth and just beyond it a toad-like man lay upon a mountain of red and yellow pillows. He wore a toga with a broad purple border. He was clean-shaven, black curls framing his portly face, with a laurel wreath wrapped around his head and tucked neatly behind his ears.

Screams, maddening screams of torture and pain echoed in the room. He searched for their origin as he wondered if he was dreaming or not, but the heat radiating from the floor through the soles of his shoes went beyond vivid sensory input. To his right, a rock wall face; to his left, a row of stone pillars spaced at arm's length apart. The edge of the floor dropped away just beyond the pillars; with no other horizontal line in his field of vision, he could only assume the screams came from the pit they appeared to be hovering over.

"John Mohr, I presume," said the bulbous man. The fat draped around his neck reverberated as he spoke.

How does he know my name? he thought as the black cat walked toward the man. "Yes," he finally said, "and you are?"

"Typical." The man flipped his hand in the air as if dismissing him. "Your race has disregarded the old gods, yet you give your loyal pet my namesake."

The black cat meowed and rubbed against the man's tree-trunk legs. The motion caused the fat to roll up and over the cat's back and John found himself waiting to see if the cat would be crushed under the weight.

"Pluto?"

"Very good."

That would mean . . . "This is Hell?"

"That depends on your point of view. To me, it is paradise." He clapped his hands together and two shambling corpses, in ill-fitting drabs, stepped out from behind the red curtain draped behind the god of the underworld. They each carried a platter of fruit and presented their wares to their master, who carefully inspected each piece as if the very universe hung in the balance of his decision.

This is maddening, John thought as he struggled to determine the sex of the creatures. Their eyes were opaque, soulless orbs, their muscles withered, and skin dehydrated and sucked tightly to their bones with long, straggly strands of white hair.

Finally, Pluto plucked the largest pomegranate from one of the trays and brought it to his puffy lips. As he bit into the fruit—skin and all—juice oozed from the corners of his mouth and ran down his double chin, disappearing into the folds of his toga.

Vile pig, John thought.

"Mind your tongue," Pluto said with a wrinkled brow. "Do not forget your place."

"You can read my thoughts?"

"But of course." He took another bite. "You would certainly indulge and let yourself go, too, if you were forced to be apart from the one you love, or, perhaps not." Pluto narrowed his eyes as his cheeks puffed out. "What would a man who married out of convenience and a hunger for social status rather than for love know of my plight?"

The myth of the seasons came into John's recollection, how a broken heart turned spring into fall. "You speak of . . . Proserpina?"

"Don't you dare speak her name, filthy creature! Her beauty is far beyond the reach of any mortal man."

"Forgive me," John said, fearing to incur Hell's wrath.

Pluto forced a smile. "Where are my manners? You must be parched." He waved his hand as to call forth another servant. John could not take his eyes off his pudgy fingers as they wriggled in the air.

Another servant stepped out from behind the man. John smelled the Scotch's aroma wafting from the goblet upon her tray. Like an old friend, it called to him. He reached for it and gazed upon the soulless creature proffering it and recognized the face, despite the concaved cheeks and vacant stare.

"Madeline?"

"Yes," Pluto said with a smile so wide it pushed the fat of his cheeks over his line of vision. "I'd like to thank you for my newest servant."

John swallowed hard, pushing the bile back down as he retracted his hand. He could not accept the drink, for he knew it was the direct cause of Madeline's current state. She was nothing more than a shadow of her former self: her once blue eyes, colorless; her blonde hair as white as the snow on a winter's morning; and her ample rosy cheeks, dull and flat. The crevice in her forehead was prominent, reminding him of that most heinous of nights and the brutality he was capable of committing.

"What have you done to her?" he asked.

Pluto sucked in a deep breath; with his eyes wide he placed his hand upon his bosom. "Me?" he said, stretching the word as if offended. "Was it not you, who in a fit of rage cleaved her head in two? You, who concealed her body behind a faux wall of your basement? You, who guiltily knocked on the wall, because you secretly wished to be caught?"

John's head lowered in shame. "Yes."

"When will you finally accept responsibility for your own actions?"

"How did Madeline come to such a place? She was a kind and generous soul."

"Indeed she was. Unfortunately, that too, is your doing. While you were off drinking yourself into a stupor, she sought the comfort of another."

"No," he said. *That's not possible. She was loyal to me.*

"Yes, she kept your secrets, but that didn't make her loyal. She was a whore who spread her legs for any man who gave her the slightest affection, because you were too busy swimming at the bottom of a bottle."

"You, shut your filthy mouth." Blinded by rage, John charged headlong, fist raised above his head, ready to pound away the mound of fat one hate-filled punch at a time.

Pluto held out his hand and the air before John rippled. His momentum stopped as if by an invisible wall and then he was suddenly sent hurling backward. He crashed on his backside to the floor. An indescribable heat radiated from the ground and he quickly stood, thanking the soles of his shoes for their protection.

"Another outburst like that and you'll be joining your Madeline by my side." Then, as if in afterthought, "And there are worse charges than catering to me, I assure you."

John's hands curled in rage. His fingernails dug deep into the soft flesh of his hands and drew blood. "Why have you forsaken me?"

"Again, you are pointing the finger in the wrong direction. Will you stop blaming the drink, the cat, and whatever unnamed demon that haunts you? Embrace the child who amused himself by tormenting those less fortunate, the young man who pushed his cousin down the stairs so that he may be the only heir to his grandfather's wealth. For that is the John Mohr whom I seek."

"How do you —"

"I know, intimately, all mortals who are destined to serve me. I've brought you here to make you an offer. I need a man with your penchant for violence."

"For what purpose?"

"Selfish reasons, of course. As your race matures, your life expectancy has increased. And at the same time, so has your lust for power and disregard for life. Never have I had so many souls bequeathed to me, but I have received fewer servants since the turn of the century, and without a war, well, I need you to offset that balance."

"And if I refuse?"

Behind John, a whip cracked, followed by searing pain as the whip split the skin on his back. The force of the blow knocked him forward to his knees. Another crack and he was on all fours. Tears rolled off his face and fell to the floor where they evaporated. He leaned back, unable to resist the pain from touching the hot floor.

Pluto held up his hand as if to stop a third assault. "Refuse, and the pain you feel right now will pale in comparison to the pain you will suffer 'til the end of time."

As he stood, John twisted his head around to see a figure standing in the shadows. It stepped forward, into the light, so that he might see his tormentor. His eyes went wide at the sight of a naked, red-skinned hulk with large, outspread bat-like wings. The creature stood proud, its broad shoulders stiff, and arched back; its muscular chest pushed outward, the whip dangling at its side ready to tear into John's flesh on command. Two gnarled horns protruded from its forehead, parallel with the floor, and its eyes glowed with Hellfire.

"It would appear as though I have no choice," John said as he stood.

Pluto signaled for the demonic creature to leave. John watched it vanish into the darkness.

"What is it you would have me do?" John asked.

"I grow bored with seeing the same servants. I desire fresh faces. I charge you with the duty to deliver the wicked to me so I may put them to better use."

"And how am I supposed to accomplish that?"

"By embracing the monster within, the monster that shows himself when you are inebriated. Pluto will guide you."

He locked gazes with the infernal beast. Its purring increased in volume until it rose over the torturous screams emanating from the pit.

Anything but that, he thought.

"That's the deal. Take it or leave it."

John stared into the soulless eyes of his former lover. There was nothing of her that remained in that hollow husk. She just stood there waiting for her next order. "I'll do it."

CHAPTER FOUR

John Mohr found himself surrounded by iron bars once more. The daylight filtering in between the iron bars of the window was like daggers to his eyes.

I was gone for half the night? he wondered. *They'll be coming for me soon.*

The black cat meowed as it passed between the bars of his jail cell.

"Wait! I am to be hung today. We had an agreement." He chased after it.

The cat ignored him and carried on its merry way.

"Come back here!" John pressed his body against the bars of his cage and reached an arm out. "Fine, then, I don't need you!"

"Settle down," said the jailer as he approached, carrying a tray of food—his last meal. "Back away from the bars."

John pursed his lips and did as instructed. He stepped all the way back to the far wall and the jailer unlocked his cell door, opened it a crack, and slid the tray inside.

"Bon Appétit!" he said with that toothy grin.

"Thank you," John said, stepping toward the food. He looked it over. "You think me a savage? How am I supposed to eat without proper utensils?"

"I may not be educated like yourself, but I ain't dumb either. Use what God gave you." The jailer wiggled his fingers then walked away.

John's stomach growled. He looked down. There, upon the tray, he found a thick steak, two eggs over easy, a biscuit and some fresh cut fruit: apples and pears. He lifted the tray and took it to his cot where he sat with it on his lap. *The indignity*, he thought as he lifted the steak to his mouth with his bare hands. With a sigh, he bit into the steak and ripped off a piece. *Cooked to perfection*, he thought as he chewed, then helped himself to another bite.

When he was finished, the jailer returned with a set of shackles as well as an escort. "It's time," he said coldly.

John nodded and stood, arms out before him and palms up. The two jailers stepped inside his cell and while one secured the shackles around his wrist and ankles, the other stood rigid, six-shooter at the ready.

In chains, John was brought outside, pulled like an animal before the growing crowd.

"We've gathered here today to see justice served," said the magistrate as John walked to the gallows.

The chains were taut, causing him to slouch forward as he walked. All eyes were upon him. Several onlookers gawked and snickered. Others pointed, booed and hissed.

Enough of this! he thought, then stopped short, pulling the chains so he might walk straight with dignity.

A woman gasped; a man shoved his son behind him as if John could break free from his bonds and wring the boy's neck; the jailer turned and scowled, but nodded as if understanding. Even with their pace slower, there was no changing the fact that with each step, John drew closer to his death.

Once on the hanging platform, the jailer pointed to the spot he needed John to stand on. *This is it.* He swallowed hard, then stepped onto the drop floor.

As the noose was draped around his neck, the magistrate said: "John Mohr, you have been tried and convicted of the murder of your wife, Madeline Mohr, on March 10th, 1842 by the Commonwealth of Virginia. On this, the 18th of September 1842, you are hereby sentenced to hang until you are dead. Do you have any final words?"

John peered through the crowd. He looked past their accusatory stares in search of the thing that put his life on such a hellacious path, but the foul beast was nowhere to be seen. He stood straight—proud. There was *no* deal, he realized. The vision he had seen was just another hallucination of his chemically-unbalanced mind. He caught the penetrating stares of two men; their wrinkled brows, pursed lips, and clenched fists revealed to him they were some of the men Pluto alluded to. He committed their faces to memory, though he was no longer sure he'd get the chance to punish them for bedding his wife.

"Very well," said the magistrate as John stood silent. He rolled up the parchment he read from and looked John dead in the eyes. "Executioner, carry out the order."

With the sound of the floorboards falling away and the squeaking of the hinges, John's body plummeted. His momentum stopped abruptly and there was tightness around his trachea. His body went rigid with the blocking of his jugular vein and carotid arteries. The noose failed to snap his neck and grant him a swift death. Realizing there was still a chance, his fingers clawed at the rope in hopes of letting in slack, but the knot remained steadfast and in the struggle he only managed to tear away his tender skin. His legs thrashed unwieldy as his body fought for survival, expending precious energy. Sparkles of light danced in his vision as his brain was denied fresh blood.

His limbs went torpid before the pain ebbed and the crowd of somber faces disappeared into the encroaching darkness.

Moments later, the darkness receded and John found himself staring into his own dead eyes. He barely recognized himself through the grime; the full beard, the long, straggly hair. The jailers refused to allow him to shave, afraid he would slit his throat and bleed out before justice could be served.

"Cut him down," ordered the magistrate.

John turned to face the crowd and realized he was floating several feet off the ground. *What madness is this?* he questioned as the crowd dispersed. *Where are they going? It's over? I'm dead?* He looked down at his ghostly body and saw straight through to the ground.

"Get the wagon," said the jailer with bad teeth to the other.

"You get it while I cut him down."

"No. We should do it together."

"Nah!" The man whipped out a pocket knife and began cutting the rope. John watched as his body fell upon its lifeless legs and crumpled to the ground.

Ruffians! he thought.

"Hey, that's disrespectful!" one jailer said.

"He's dead. Besides, he murdered his wife. He don't deserve no respect. Now go get the cart!"

John wished for nothing more than to reach out and grab hold of the man's throat; wanted to make himself corporal before the man's eyes and watch as all the color drained from the man's face as fear hugged him in its cold embrace.

As if struck by a hurricane force wind, John was propelled backward. He frantically waved his arms in an effort to slow his progression, but it proved fruitless. As he swooshed through the air, he passed the courthouse with its wood-shingled roof, brick walls and corbel cornice, and the neighboring clerk's house under the auspices. He passed through a chimney haunch of a small, stone coble residential home, and through the beaded clapboard of another home, taking notice of the carved interior door facings. He exited out its four rock chimney, then passed over the tavern where he had spent far too many nights rather than at home with his wife and pets, and past an apartment building into the adjacent alley. His body finally stopped when he came upon the black cat gorging itself on a large street rat.

Even in death I cannot escape this damnable beast, he thought as he hovered over its shoulder. *When will my suffering end?*

When the cat was finished with its meal, it walked through the alleyways of Bigler's Mill. Though John had no inclination to follow the one-eyed beast, his intangible body drifted along as if connected to the creature by an invisible umbilical cord, yet the beast paid him no mind. He followed the cat's fancy, and they travelled throughout the small Virginia town until finally, nightfall, and the cat stopped its nonsensical behavior and returned to the gallows.

The jailers had left John's body on the cart some thirty feet away from the gallows—left it out in the sun to rot and for the crows to feast—the pinkish color already drained out of his face, the shimmer in his eyes gone, clouded over by death. If he had working shoulders, surely they would have twitched at the purple-red ring around his neck, a permanent reminder of the evil in his heart.

How could they leave my body out in the open like this for all manner of beasts? Lazy, good for nothing, sons of— The cat gracefully leapt onto the cart. It crawled up John's leg and perched itself atop his chest.

What is it doing?

He watched as the beast kneaded its paws against the lifeless chest as if performing some sort of morbid ritual. The cat craned its neck and exhaled a blue fog with veins of white pulsating through it. The breath passed over the corpse's lips and in the blink of an eye, John's spirit rushed forward, pulled by an unseen force toward his rotting carcass.

CHAPTER FIVE

Slowly, John's eyes fluttered open to the sight of the full moon perched high in the sky, his mind encompassed by pins-and-needles-like pain. His stomach ached to the point he felt the need to curl himself into the fetal position to alleviate it.

"You certainly took your time," he said to the black cat upon his chest. "I thought I was trapped in that ghastly state forever."

The cat turned away as if snubbing him, then leapt off his chest and over the edge of the cart he found himself lying on. He sat upright, joints stiff and creaky.

Meow!

He turned his head to the right, a motion that took more effort than he could have imagined, and looked at the cat. *Strange,* he thought, seeing the patch of white was no longer isolated to its breast, but now extended the full length of its belly.

"What is it?" he asked.

The cat took several steps ahead, then turned and meowed once more.

The god of the underworld's voice echoed in his mind. *Pluto will guide you.*

"Fine. We'll play it your way, for now."

After scooting himself to the bottom of the cart, John stood and took his first step as the undead. With each step the effects of rigor mortis dissipated and his movements became less sluggish and more controlled. He stepped toward the cat, a part of him wanting nothing more than to snatch it up and wring its neck and finally be free of the accursed beast, but the other part was too afraid, and so he acceded and followed the cat through the streets of Bigler's Mill.

The streets were barren, but the cat kept John in the shadows. When they passed the tavern, his stomach protested. He longed to join in the drunken revelry sounding from within and sip on a glass of scotch, but he knew should he be caught, he'd be burned at the stake as a heretic. The tavern's patrons would surely beat and drag him through the streets before setting him a blaze. After all, no one came back from the dead.

Would I survive the fire? Could I be brought back once more? Would I want to be after such a violent end?

Meow!

"All right," he whispered, but with a coarse tone. "I'm coming."

John followed the cat to the edge of town, to a small farm that grew peanuts and tomatoes. With no buildings to slink behind, he used the deciduous, broad leaf oak trees for cover. The farmhouse was a small, one story home the lower half made of cobble stone, and the upper of beaded clapboard. Smoke snaked into the air from the brick chimney, signaling the Peters were home.

As he drew closer to the farmhouse, he wondered why no aromas permeated his senses. Whether the Peters were cooking or not, the smoke wafting into the night air should have held at least an oak or hickory scent. Not even dung of the livestock could be smelled. Then he realized he felt no external sensations. The nearby trees and shrubs swayed, but the wind offered him no gentle caress.

What has happened to me?

Shouting from inside the farmhouse broke his train of thought and he continued on the path set forth by the black cat. On his way he plucked a tomato off the vine and sank his teeth into it; its juices filled his mouth.

"Gah! Vile!" He spit it out and inspected the fruit, expecting to find it rotten . . . but it was perfectly ripened. He dropped the tomato and raked his fingers across his tongue. *What the . . .* He looked at his fingers, surprised by their tasty flavor. *Could it be?*

The cat meowed, drawing his attention back to the task at hand and led him to a window where inside he could see Thomas Peters screaming at his wife, arms raised and sawing in the air. The fear was etched on her face, her head sunk into her shoulders and chin tucked into her bosom as if she had already been struck once and feared another blow.

John looked down at the cat and asked, "Him?"

It purred and rubbed against his leg. He could not remember the last time the animal showed such affection. At the same time, he could not be certain this was indeed affection or a ploy to earn his trust, or even just its way of saying yes.

A loud thwack stole his attention from the cat. He turned in time to see Emma Peters stumble forward, and her husband reeling for another blow. The sight stirred emotions long buried under alcohol.

Is this what abuse looks like? Is this what Madeline was forced to endure all because she said "I do"?

A hunger unlike any he had known in life gripped him. Rage boiled inside his cold veins as Emma was forced to the floor. Thomas bent at the knees to strike her for the third time, and John had seen enough. He made his way toward the front door. It was open and he stepped inside. Emma's cries gave his dead feet a sense of urgency.

When John reached the living room, where the all too familiar violence was taking place, Emma was crab-crawling backward away from Thomas, her eyes wide with fear. Thomas grabbed hold of the coffee table blocking his path and tossed it aside. She screamed and flinched at the sound of it crashing to the floor. John snuck up behind Thomas and Emma's eyes proved she saw him, but said nothing, unknowingly exchanging one monster for another.

John grabbed Thomas by the shoulders and pulled him close.

"What the.... Who the hell are you?"

The only question John sought an answer for was how to dispatch of this wretch. The throbbing veins pulsing under the skin of the man's neck drummed in John's ears stirring something primal. A mounting ache consumed his rational mind and he lost himself.

Mad with hunger, John leaned in ad libitum. Before the man had a chance to react, John sank his teeth into the side of the man's throat. Blood sprayed the inside of his mouth and it was a warm welcome to his cold, rotting flesh.

"Let go!" Thomas demanded as he struggled to break free.

Feeding the urge, John's awareness returned and with it his true purpose. *It tastes so good. Unlike anything that has ever crossed these lips before.*

John wrestled Thomas to the ground, biting, tearing, and swallowing each piece of flesh so as to claim another. Emma screamed one last time before standing and running away. He tracked the sound of her footsteps to the kitchen, then heard a door slam.

The room filled with Thomas's agonizing screams as his flesh was ripped asunder. "Why are you doing this?" he asked in between gasps as he was finally able to push John's chomping teeth away from his neck and shoulder in his distraction.

"Because there's a place in the darkest pit of Hell for you. The god of the underworld was impressed by the malice in my mind and I was chosen as your executioner," he said, then leaned in for another bite. "And your flesh is unlike anything I've ever tasted. The sweetest of cured meats pales in comparison."

With both hands pressed against John's chest, Thomas was able to keep him at bay. However, blood pumped out of the wounds already inflicted and the color of his cheeks faded. Soon, he wouldn't have the strength to fight and John's hunger would finally be satiated.

Just have to keep the pressure on, he thought.

John bore his thumb into an open wound and Thomas unleashed a blood-curdling scream. The elbow buckled under the pain and John made his move. Blood dripped from the appendage as he quickly pulled it out from the warm flesh and shoved Thomas's arm to the floor, pinning it as he leaned in and clamped his teeth around the front of the man's throat. With the flesh pinched between his teeth, he pulled back. Tendons and veins popped as they were yanked out. Blood geysered, showering John in crimson rain.

Thomas choked on the flowing river of blood. Small bubbles formed and burst with each gurgle. John leaned back and watched with a morbid curiosity as the life slipped away from his fellow abuser. With a soft sigh, Thomas's life faded. With his immortal soul now delivered to his master, John hoisted Thomas's left arm to his mouth and began to feast.

CHAPTER SIX

The minutes passed by seamlessly as John gorged himself on the flesh of his victim. No matter how many bites he slipped past his lips, the hunger was relentless, but once the body was cold, it no longer appeased him.

The idea of eating human meat would sicken any rational mind, he thought as he stared down at the carnage he created. *Why is it I have no qualms about it? Pluto, what did you do to me? And why won't this hunger abate?*

Remembering Emma was in the other room, he stood and made his way toward her.

The cat appeared from out of nowhere and blocked his path.

"Out of the way," he said with the wave of his arm. "She's a witness."

The cat arched its back. The hairs went ridged, and it hissed its displeasure.

"I don't understand," he said.

The cat hissed again and took a step toward him. He stepped backward and the cat stepped closer.

"All right. I get the idea. We're leaving."

He didn't like leaving Emma alive and well, knowing she had seen his face. It wouldn't be long after he was gone that she would run to her closest neighbor and tell her horrific story. *Surely they'll form a lynch mob*, he thought as he and the cat exited the house.

The cat bounded out in front of him, turned, and meowed. He nodded and followed. They walked through the farmland and back into town. The moon was high in the sky, illuminating the streets. The lights were out in all the residential homes and John couldn't help but wonder where or to whom the cat was leading him.

They happened across the tavern, but before he could get excited about the prospect of a drink, the cat ducked down the alleyway. In the darkness, a glass shattered and a curse word was uttered. The cat vanished into the shadows and John could only assume this was his next target. He too kept to the shadows as he made his way between the buildings.

A belch echoed in the night followed by an "excuse me" and John couldn't help but wonder how many he would have to face. With his muscles still tight, could he handle a fight with multiple adversaries?

I barely over-powered Thomas. Perhaps their inebriation will prove to my benefit, he thought.

A man stumbled out of the darkness and into John's line of sight.

"Hey, buddy, got a drink?"

John peered into the darkness and saw no one else.

"Hey! I'm talking to you. You deaf?"

"No," John said, taking a step toward him. "Just hungry."

He lunged forward. The man threw his arms up to protect himself, but he was knocked to the ground. Before tearing into the man's flesh with his teeth, John looked to the cat for approval. The cat turned its head away and John needed nothing more than that. He leaned in and ripped the man's nose off with a single bite. The man's hands shot toward his face to cover his wound as John chewed the morsel.

The autumn air had given the fellow's exposed skin an unappetizing chill. Seeking warmer meat, John plunged his hand into the man's abdomen and yanked out a kidney. As he brought it to his lips, the kidney slipped between his fingers, but before he could recover and taste it, the man reached out and grabbed hold of John's wrist. For a dying man, John was surprised by the strength exuded against him. They struggled over the piece of gore until finally, the loss of blood proved too much. The man's hand slowly slipped away and fell lifelessly to his side.

Victorious, John sank his teeth into the kidney and reveled in its exquisite taste. He devoured it, licked his fingers clean, then reached in and rummaged for the other kidney before the body grew cold.

It wasn't long before the body lost its heat and shortly after that, John lost his interest in it. The cat meowed and he knew it was time to leave.

"Where to now?" he asked, not expecting an answer.

The cat walked out of the alley and he followed. As he passed a window, he caught his reflection in the glass. He stopped and stared at his bloodstained chin and cheeks, the blood dry and cracked.

Finally, the monster within shows itself, he thought. *Perhaps this was me all along. A savage beast.* Disgusted by the sight of himself, he rammed his fist through the single-pane glass. Cut and torn, he pulled his hand back through. There was no pain, no blood. Just lacerations, some deep, some shallow with tiny shards of glass clinging to his undead flesh.

A light inside the building turned on. "Who's there?" came a voice.

His stomach growled, still not satisfied, but the cat hissed. *Will I ever be content?* he wondered as he looked down at his gut. *Or is this my curse? My penance?* As quickly as he was able, he darted off, the cat leading the way.

Soon the sun would rise and the people of Bigler's Mill would be up and about attending to their remedial chores. While the men attended to the livestock, chopped wood, and hunted for the night's meal, the women would busy themselves with the previous day's laundry, cooking, and seeing to the children.

And what shall I be doing? he wondered as he continued to walk. The cat led him to the other side of town. *What are we doing out here, the only thing in this direction is . . .* Off in the distance he saw the garden cemetery behind the church.

Is my work done? Is this to be my final resting place?

They passed under the iron arch of the gate. The graveyard floor was covered with a low blanket of fog. He looked around at the small, wooden crosses marking the graves of those less fortunate. Those citizens who didn't have the money to pay for a marble or granite headstone were allocated—tightly— to the surrounding perimeter of the cemetery away from the shadier plots. As they walked the manicured path deeper into the cemetery, the headstones and grave markers became more elaborate. Looking ahead on the path, John had no idea where the cat was taking him, or for what reason.

Am I to exhume a corpse? Is my next victim living among the dead?

They stopped at a mausoleum. The cat meowed and passed between the iron bars of the crypt's door. John looked over the elaborate structure, its fluted stone columns, ornate ironwork, and the ivy creeping halfway up the stonewall. His gaze drifted to the plaque mounted to the right of the door.

"Henken," he said, recognizing the family name. A fellow bank officer he had worked with in life.

He reached out and tugged on the padded lock attached to the chain. *Well, I simply cannot pass through the bars. What to do?* His head swiveled right to left as he looked around the cemetery for something heavy. *Nothing but grave markers and headstones.* Not wanting to desecrate his dead brethren, he continued on the path, hoping to find a simple rock to smash the lock.

Moonlight reflected off something metallic in the distance and he squinted his eyes to see it.

Perfect!

Just over a grassy hill was an open grave, the handle of a shovel nestled in a mound of freshly turned soil. By the time he reached the top of the hill, a pinkish-hue appeared on the horizon from the rising sun. He snatched the shovel and returned to the Henken family crypt.

He struck the lock with the shovel, but it remained steadfast. He hacked at it several more times until finally it disengaged. Not wanting to draw attention to the gate or its lock, he returned the shovel to the mound of dirt before entering the sepulchre.

As the sun peeked over the horizon, John was finally ready to catch up with the cat. The rusty hinges creaked as he swung the door open. He peered through the darkness and waited just a second before realizing how silly he was being. He was already dead and there was no need for trepidation. What could hurt him? He walked down the stone steps and into the brick-lined underground space. In the center of the room resided a stone coffin, the final resting place for the patriarch of the family. In the wall immediately to the right were two small children entombed with plaques reading: IN LOVING MEMORY, with dates of birth and death.

"Such a shame, really. Neither reached five years of age."

The cat jumped atop the stone coffin and meowed. He turned and looked at the beast.

"What is it you want from me?"

The cat jumped down and headed for the stairs. He followed, but the cat turned and hissed.

"Damn you, wretched beast. Fine. I'll stay," he said, realizing what it wanted. "Leave me, then."

The cat darted off without looking back.

So that's it? I'm to stay here out of sight, and out of the sun. I suppose the coolness of the crypt will preserve my addling body. John looked around the damp, dark crypt. His stomach growled, the only pain his dead body felt keeping him company until nightfall.

CHAPTER SEVEN

With nothing but his thoughts to keep him company, John ruminated about the life he led that put him in this dire predicament. He sat in the far corner; the sunlight that filtered into the sepulchre through the iron bars pained his eyes, the rays like tiny needles through the soft tissue.

He thought of Madeline and how he only asked for her hand in marriage when he heard he wouldn't be entitled to his inheritance until he was in a position to carry on the family name. With his grandfather's fading health and his own father dead, John Mohr was the last living male after pushing his cousin down the stairs and calling it an accident. His grandfather refused to give him a single cent until he was married and thus he and Madeline were wed at the age of sixteen. Shortly after their nuptials, his grandfather finally lost his battle with cholera and John had thought the pressure to have children died along with him. They moved into his estate where they were happy for a time, but soon, the house's empty rooms and halls weighed heavily on Madeline's heart. Unable to satisfy his wife, or his grandfather's dying wish, he turned to the bottle and consequently destroyed all he had planned for.

She was so beautiful, so innocent, and yet he destroyed that innocence without batting an eye. *At least in death I finally have a reason for not achieving an erection*, he thought as he listened to the silence of his heart. A rat scurried across the room and began to tug at his pant leg's bottom, distracting him from his thoughts.

Two more rats came out of a nearby hole; their squeaks were like nails on a chalkboard to his ears. *They're hungry*, he thought, looking at the one tugging on his pants. He snatched it up and brought it closer to his face. The vermin bit down on his index finger, but John felt nothing. Still, the deed irritated him further. The thought of eating it, swallowing it whole, crossed his mind. Instead, he snapped the critter's neck and tossed the carcass to its brethren. Though he was above eating filth, the other two rats weren't about to let a meal go to waste. They dragged it back into their den and left him alone to his devices and for a brief moment he wondered how many mouths needed feeding within the darkness of that tiny hole.

An image of his cousin, Frank, flashed in his mind's eye. *What would he have grown up to be?* he wondered. The boy did poorly in his studies and certainly would have had to enter an apprenticeship in order to become a contributing member of society. John always felt Frank was holding him back because their private tutor spent hours repeating the lessons.

They had just finished with their studies for the day and were heading up the stairs to return their leather ledgers to their respective bedrooms. John made it to the top first and suddenly turned around, holding out his hand. Frank ran into the palm and tumbled backwards. By the time he landed on the floor, his neck was broken in two places. No one could imagine it was murder and thus John was alone to learn all he could. He excelled in math and had a firm grasp of language.

Tired of reminiscing and remembering why he was in the predicament he was in, he closed his eyes, thinking he could sleep, but instead he saw the outside world passing by. *What in the name of—* His eyes opened to the stone coffin perched in the center of the crypt. *This is too fantastical,* he thought, closing his eyes again to see the legs of people rushing by. Given the fact he could see no higher than their knees, he assumed he was seeing the world through the cat's eye.

The creature he loathed now was an intimate part of him.

Curious, his eyes remained closed and he watched the cat travel along with no one paying it any mind. A crowd of people were gathered in the streets, directly in front of the alley where John slaughtered the drunk.

"That's what Emma Peters said happened to her husband. Said it was John Mohr's ghost who dunnit."

"She's crazy if she saw Mohr," said a man with his hands on his hips.

"No. His body went missing last night."

"Could just be some of the youngins foolin' around, but more than likely, an animal dragged it off into the woods."

"I don't know."

"Yeah, he could have survived."

"No one's survived a hangin' before."

"Did you see the bruise on Emma's face?" asked one of the ladies. "Thomas walloped her good. Poor dear probably has no idea what she saw."

"Agreed," said one of the men. "This is the work of an animal, wolves more than likely. No doubt in my mind."

The cat passed under a gown, between a pair of legs and out the other side. The woman jumped up, startled, but chuckled after seeing the cat stalk down the alleyway. The cat had stopped and turned around when the woman screeched, and all John could think of was for the feral beast to carry on its merry way and put some distance between itself and the cacophony of the crowd. But it stayed behind and watched, revealing the scene to John. The body of John's victim lay face up right where he had left it.

"Move aside . . . move aside."

The cat turned to see an officer push his way through the crowd with the aid of his baton.

"Dear Lord in Heaven," he said, removing his helmet in respect for the dead. He turned back around to face the crowd. "All right, clear out of here. We're going to need to get the wagon in here. Move along." He shooed the people.

"I'd like to know what you're doing about this," someone said.

"Yeah," several others in the crowd added.

"A curfew has been issued and we've sent word to Richmond requesting more men. If need be, we'll deputize some of the men in town until the outlaw has been incarcerated. Now, please, move along."

The mob dispersed, but whispers were still heard. Those who hung back as the law-abiding citizens pushed their way out of the crowd were threatened with a walloping from the baton.

The officer turned back to the alley and locked gazes with the cat. "Oh no you don't. That ain't your next meal. Git!" He stomped his foot in the cat's direction. It hissed, but then darted off.

John continued to stay in the cat's perspective as it traveled through the town. At first he enjoyed the sensation of secretly spying on the townspeople, but soon his excitement turned to rage. Seeing the people the cat passed by only increased his stomach's displeasure with remaining in the shadows, rather than being out feasting. Suddenly, as if sensing John's thoughts, the cat turned around. It ran into the street, straight at a horse and wagon and John hoped to see the cat's head crushed by one of the horse's hooves, or caught in the spokes of a wagon wheel, but it weaved in between the horse's legs with an unnatural agility and continued its return to the cemetery.

It passed through the iron gate entrance of the cemetery, bolted past the mausoleum where he was hiding, and up the grassy hill to where John had found the open grave. The cat crept to the edge of the grave and peered inside to see an old man on top of the open casket. Inside was the body of a young woman whom John did not recognize.

Stealing from the dead, how low, John thought, witnessing the sacrilegious deed.

The old man pocketed a necklace with a locket in his overalls. As the old man closed the casket, the cat stepped back and hid before he climbed out of the grave. When the man started to sling dirt into the pit, the cat stepped out from behind the headstone.

Meow!

"Well, lookie here," said the man as he drove the shovel into the dirt and leaned against it. "You lost, kitty? Oh! Look at that eye. That must've been some fight."

The cat sat and licked its front paw, then rubbed it against the side of its face.

"Trying to be cute to get some of my lunch, hey? Well . . . it worked. You hungry? I got some cured ham you're welcome to." The man stepped toward the nearby tree where John noticed a knapsack balled up in the shade.

The cat turned and walked away.

"Hey, where you goin'?"

As if ignoring the man, hoping to lure him, the cat continued to walk.

That's it, lead him back here, John thought as he stood and concealed himself in the corner where the penetrating sunlight could not reach.

"Come back, kitty!"

Meow! The cat bolted down the stairs.

No longer seeing through the cat's eye, John waited.

"Hey, why's this lock open. Who's there? Damn kids. I'm gonna tan your hide!"

Foolishly, without a lantern or his shovel, the old man walked down the stairs and into the open crypt. "Where you hidin'? Come on out of there."

When the gravekeeper stepped past where John was concealed, John grabbed hold of him and bit down on the side of his neck in one fluid motion. The weathered skin was dry and tough. The old man pulled himself free, hand clutching the wound.

Before he could turn around to see his assailant, John shoved him from behind. The old man stumbled and lost his footing. With his hand at his neck he was unable to protect himself from the fall. The stone corner slammed into the left side of his face and tore open his skull as his momentum carried him to the floor. Blood pooled at the base of the stone pedestal, accenting the gothic atmosphere where the coffin sat atop it.

John threw himself on top of the body, ravenously biting and clawing. He eyed the cracked cranium and wondered about the meat inside. He probed the wound's edges but could not pluck a morsel to taste.

I'll have to widen the hole, he thought. He grabbed the head by the silver hair, craned the neck back, and slammed it down onto the brick floor. It hit with a wet *smack,* but little extra damage was done. *Not enough.*

After dragging the corpse to the middle of the room, he searched the man's pockets for the stolen locket. Once found, he held it up into the light and opened the clasp. Inside was a photo of the young woman with a young man and a baby nestled between them—a memento to keep her company until they were reunited in the afterlife.

"What a lovely family." To the man, "You should be ashamed of yourself. How many others have you stolen from?"

Disgusted, he pocketed the locket and pushed the stone lid off the coffin and over the edge. He surprised himself with the strength exerted from his dead muscles. *A gift from Pluto*, he wondered. The corner of the lid crashed down first, hitting the back of the old man's skull with pinpoint accuracy. Bone collapsed under the weight and brain matter splashed outward.

"Ah!" he said with boyish glee. He stooped down on his knees and collected the spongy tissue from the floor. He brought the tantalizing meat to his lips and sank his teeth in. "Delicious." He licked his cracked lips with a half-rotten tongue, then pushed the coffin's lid off his prey. The skull was completely smashed, as well as the meat inside, but it made no difference to him for it still tasted the same.

Once the cranium was devoid of all content, he tore into the man's stomach and wrestled with his small intestine. The viscera squished in his hands and stretched as he tried to take a bite. It popped and squirted its juices over his face, further matting his beard. He took notice of the eyeball dangling from its socket, plucked it from the nerve endings and tossed it into his gullet as if it was a grape. It burst between his teeth, liquid filling his mouth. He swallowed it, barely tasting it, then dug out the other.

By the time he finished devouring his favorite parts, the body had lost all of its heat. Though he was still hungry, the taste of cold flesh didn't sit well with him. He looked down at his growling stomach to see it bulging over his pants.

Pluto has made me gluttonous, just like him, he thought, pursing his lips. *Best to just take my mind off the hunger. A distraction is what I need.*

He walked up the stairs, the sunlight bright and painful to behold. With his hand over his brow, he peeked outside the iron bars of the crypt.

This isn't going to work, he thought, turning around. *The pain is too much.*

Even with his eyes closed, the sun's harshness was unavoidable. He returned to his shady corner of the crypt; giving the locket to its rightful owner would have to wait.

CHAPTER EIGHT

When night finally fell, John left the safety of the crypt and headed for the open grave—at least he hoped it was still an open grave, or else he'd have to dig it up if he was going to return the locket. The cat protested all the way, but his determination won out and the cat followed him for a change.

At the top of the grassy hill, he was relieved to see no one else had come along to cover the gravesite. He hopped inside and opened the lid. The young maiden was lovely, untouched by decay or disease, but her cheeks were starting to concave. John couldn't help but wonder what had claimed her life. There was no pebbly, dry rash caused by Scarlet Fever or any other physical signs of sickness. *Maybe it was tuberculosis. Her cheeks could be a sign of consumption.*

He pulled the necklace out of his pocket and leaned forward. "I apologize for the disturbance," he said as he slung the gold chain around her neck. "May you finally rest in peace."

With the pine box closed, he climbed out of the grave and buried her under the mound of soil.

"All right then," he said, turning to the cat. "Where to? How about taking me to one of those bastards who sent Madeline to Hell?"

The cat hissed, then turned and made its way out of the cemetery and back toward town.

Temperamental beast, he thought.

Upon exiting the cemetery, and just at the outskirts of town, John noticed lantern lights in the surrounding wooded area. He slinked behind the nearest home and watched.

Must be searching for the wolves they're blaming the murders on. Perfect, he thought, then checked the streets of the town. *Deserted.*

He left the shadows and crossed the street to where the cat stood waiting by the general store. John was jealous at the ease the beast had at coming and going as it pleased. Together again, the cat darted behind the building. Once around the corner, they kept out of sight and traveled to the tavern.

A light from an open doorway illuminated the darkness. Slow and careful, John followed the cat. Peering into the doorway, the cat meowed; movement was heard from inside the building. John ducked behind a mound of broken crates, knowing it would only take one scream to bring the lynch mob out of the woods and back into town.

My meal would be cut short.

"I don't suppose you're the wild beast tormenting the town, now, are you?" asked Michael Smith, the barkeep, from within. "I'll be right back with a special treat for you."

Now's my chance, John thought as he stepped out from behind the crates and tiptoed to the edge of the doorway. As if sensing his plan, the cat stepped back three steps to force Michael out from under the doorframe.

Michael stepped outside with his right arm extended, holding a saucer of milk. "Here you go, my darlin'."

As he bent over to place the saucer before the cat, John jumped him from behind. The saucer crashed to the ground; its contents spilled. With reflexes and strength he still could not believe he had, John wrapped his arms around his prey. Left arm across Michael's chest, right across his face. With his hand at the base of Michael's chin, he twisted and yanked. The neck snapped, a popping noise echoed in his ear and Michael's body went limp in his arms. He let it drop lifelessly to the ground.

"Sorry about your treat," he said to the cat, who just stared at him with that emerald green eye.

The cat stepped toward the dish and lapped at the small amount left behind at the base of the dish. John shrugged his shoulders, not really caring one way or the other, and returned his attention to his own treat before it grew too cold for his liking.

Better drag it inside. It's not safe to tear into it out here, he thought, grabbing the carcass by the ankles. With the body inside, he closed the doors just to be safe.

Before the sound of him grunting and chewing filled the air, John walked through the kitchen and checked the bar area. Unequivocally due to the curfew, the tavern was empty of patrons. John could only imagine the difficulty of sending away all the besotted customers and he deduced Michael had gotten a late start on locking up. Since the man lived in one of the rooms he rented out upstairs, he would not be found in violation. As he walked back to the body, John noticed a collection of knives on a chopping block. He looked to his hands, bloody and raw. But the blood was not his own. The skin on his fingertips was peeling away and his fingernails were cracked and partially lifted off.

How much damage can they suffer before rotting off? He pulled the largest knife from the wood block. *Time to take a different approach.*

He carved strips of flesh from Michael's back and John did his best to make it appear as an animal attack. He left four gashes running the length of Michael's back, then flipped him over. He dug out the man's eyes with the tip of the blade and popped them into his mouth one at a time. After slicing open his abdomen, he reached in and sorted through the organs, leaving the undesirable ones strewn around the body. The colon and large intestine were two John had no desire to eat and the effort needed to chew through the liver was more trouble than it was worth.

When he was finished, he stood and noticed his distended stomach. *I'm bloated! How is this possible? It would seem I can eat, but not digest it.* With the knife still in his hand, he lifted his shirt and ran the blade across the skin, making sure to apply enough pressure to penetrate the stomach lining. Pieces of half-chewed flesh spilled onto the floor in a syrupy mess, and hidden within the gore lay a finger. Still hungry, he bent over and moved a few unappetizing pieces of flesh aside to retrieve it. As he stood, knife still in hand, he raised the severed appendage level with his eye and inspected it.

Swallowed the digit whole. His shoulder shrugged as his head cocked to the left before he nibbled off what little flesh it had to offer. Safely tucked inside his rotting flesh, the meat had some warmth. He discarded the bone and, not feeling any different, John continued on his way. He opened the back door and stepped out into the night, bumping into a constable.

"Hey . . . you're . . ." The man reached for the whistle dangling from a rope around his neck.

As the whistle drew close to the officer's lips, John slammed the palm of his hand into it, shoving the metal deep into the man's mouth. The officer coughed, releasing a half-blown whistle. Moonlight glistened off the blade as John brought it up and slashed the officer's throat. His eyes went wide with shock. Blood spilled forth like a morbid waterfall down his chest. The officer dropped to his knees.

Though John didn't want to stick around, afraid of another officer checking in on his brethren, he knew if he left the body in such a state they would surely rule out an animal attack. He dropped to all fours and buried his teeth into the man's neck. He bit, chewed, pulled and tugged until there was barely any flesh left to keep the head attached to the shoulders. He lifted his head periodically to make sure the area was still clear.

The cat stepped out from the alleyway and waltzed up to him. He grabbed it around the waist and it hissed in protest. With its paw secured in his hand, he raked its nails across the officer's cheek and hoped it would be enough to maintain the charade. Before he could release the cat, it twisted itself around in his hands and clawed the length of his forearm.

"Wretched beast!" His hands found solace around its neck and without thought, he snapped its neck in two.

A wave of relief fell over him, a calming he had never known in life, as if a huge burden had just been lifted from his shoulders. He let the beast fall to the ground and marveled at his malevolence.

No, he thought, *can't leave it here. Wouldn't want the authorities to start second-guessing themselves.*

He grabbed the cat by the tail and walked away, swinging the beast merrily with each step.

CHAPTER NINE

Inside the crypt, John was alone and hungry, and more than afraid to close his eyes and see the death he brought upon the beast. He had ditched the cat's body, leaving it for scavengers, in a pile of fallen leaves. Though the old man's half-eaten carcass still lay face down on the floor, it provided no companionship.

Maybe I should have refrained from killing Pluto? I might have hated the foul thing, but at least I wasn't alone.

"Julia, over hear. This one's open!" someone said outside the sepulchre.

Upon hearing the voice, John stood and leaned against the wall, out of sight.

"Where's old man Harris?"

"Hell if I know. C'mon."

"Maybe we shouldn't. Maybe Harris is down there?"

"Then maybe we give the old kook something to watch."

John could feel the ardor in the young man's voice and knew what he was about to bear witness to.

"Stop it," the girl giggled. "Hey!"

John then heard the distinct sound of flesh smacking against flesh and he could only assume the boy's advancement was unwarranted.

"Jeez, Julia. Did you have to hit me so hard?"

"As a matter of fact, yeah. Not out here," she said.

"Then let's go down there . . . out of sight. You promised."

"I know. All right."

The young couple's shadows cascaded on the stone stairs, stretching deeper into the sepulchre with each step. John curled his fists in anticipation.

"It looks dark," said the girl.

"Don't worry, I'm here. Nothing's going to happen that you don't want."

The girl came into the room first. "Well . . . I did promise."

"Yes, you—"

John exploded out of the shadows, slamming his body into the boy's. The girl screamed as the boy was planted against the brick wall, their scuffle blocking her exit. John sank his teeth into the back of his head and came away with a mouthful of skin and hair, but his blunt teeth could not penetrate the skull. As he chewed, he grabbed the boy's head and slammed it once more against the brick wall. The boy's face slid down the wall as his legs gave out from underneath him, and he lay unconscious at the girl's feet.

"Who are you?" she asked to no response. "Why are you doing this?"

There was no answer John could give her. This wasn't personal. Even aghast, the young woman was beautiful and it would be such a shame to sunder her from this world. Perhaps the boy would be enough to appease the craving, the deep, all-consuming ache.

"My father is very wealthy." She moved toward the exit. "I could—"

He lunged at her, hands out in front of him. That split-second of doubt, of not wanting to harm her, gone, replaced by the projection of his wife onto her. He told himself in time, she would be just like Madeline. He would save some worthless oaf the heartache. She screamed as he tore her light-blue gown. His weight crashed upon her and they fell to the floor together. He exposed her underdeveloped bosom and sank his teeth into the soft, tender meat. She wailed in agony before her hands slapped against his cheeks and she leaned in to try to pry him off her. He was too strong. Her efforts were futile.

"Get off! Jeffrey, wake up. Please help me."

John's head shot upward. He planted his lips against her and pinched her tongue between his teeth. She tried to scream, but with their lips locked it was nothing more than a muffled murmur that grew louder as more pressure was applied to the appendage. Warm, intoxicating blood pooled inside John's mouth as the girl's tongue severed. With her hands pressed against her mouth she whimpered for help.

Stealing a glance over his shoulder, John suspected the boy dead. If not now, surely he would bleed to death soon enough. His hand rocketed upward, catching the girl square in the jaw. Her head whipped back, hitting the brick floor hard. Vacantly, she stared up at the ceiling as John scooted himself lower on her body. After hoisting her dress up, he buried his head in her thigh; the meat was plump and sweet.

When he was finished, John sat in the corner, wondering if the children were destined to spend eternity in servitude to Pluto or not. *Was this the first time they were to fornicate? If so, I may have condemned them prematurely. But then if they* were *sexually active, then what else were they into?*

Movement caught his attention. He leaned to his left to see the girl's legs bend at the knees and her feet struggle for traction.

Odd, I would've sworn she was dead. Perhaps my rotting hands couldn't feel the faint pulse? He eyed her intently. *But the blood lost its warmth . . .*

He stood, ready for his second course, when he noticed her opaque eyes staring at him. She snarled as she sat up. The boy planted his palms against the floor and hoisted himself up as well. John bent forward to get a closer look at him and found the same soulless eyes staring back at him.

"This is new," he said, trying to wrap his mind around the possibility.

The couple stood and stared at him, hunger in their eyes. Their bodies swayed as they contemplated their next move.

"Well, then," John said, raising his fists and assuming a fighting stance, "I'm the one chosen by a god."

They turned toward the stone stairs and with one shaky step at a time, ascended the stairs out into the sunlight. With his arm shielding his eyes, John followed them to the entrance. He watched them shamble through the cemetery and into the neighboring woods. Unable to withstand the sun's harsh rays any longer, he returned to the crypt.

How can they walk in the day, unhindered by the sun?

As if to answer his question, the earth beneath him trembled. Dust and debris fell from the walls inside the crypt as loose stone and mortar broke free. John's arms flailed as his dead legs struggled to maintain their balance. The floor before him cracked open and the room was filled with the screams of the damned. Even with his hands over his ears he still heard their incessant pleading.

Skeletal hands reached for him through the opening, clawing at the air as he jumped backward.

Fiends! he thought, staring down at the abnormally long, bony fingers. "It's not my time!"

The floor behind him split and six arms shot upward, taking hold of him. Fingers clawed at his thighs and calves, securing themselves in his flesh before dragging him down into the crevice. He fell into darkness, the skeletons still clinging to him, struggling to climb up his legs and reach his face so they might gouge out his eyes and claim his soul as their own. Their fingertips raked his skin and burned his flesh as they continued to fall.

The pain can only mean one thing: I'm returning to Hell!

The added weight of their bones caused his body to tilt. Their bodies twisted and turned as they fell for what felt like an eternity. A skeletal hand reached for the mass of rotting flesh he called a nose and he grabbed it by the wrist. He snapped the bones back and tossed the broken hand before planting his right fist into the center of the skeleton's skull. The fiend's grip on John's flesh loosened and it fell backward, knocking one of its brethren off John's legs. The two skeletons fell together into the abyss, one smacking the other in a fitful rage. In a barrage of fists and kicks, John fended off two more.

One left, he thought as he stared into its vacant eye sockets. He reeled his right fist back and with every ounce of strength he could muster, slammed his fist into the godless creature's skull. His fingers broke on impact—searing pain ignited in his hand—but the blow proved effective. The last skeleton fell away, its arms outstretched toward John as the darkness below them consumed it and he was left alone in the descending darkness.

Heat radiated from beneath him and John prayed his fall was coming to an end. The darkness receded to an orange glow. The sound of water echoed in the chasm and John suddenly splashed into a river of silver water.

He struggled to reach the surface and when he did, the water swept him away. If he actually needed to breathe, John knew he would be dead in a matter of seconds. Gulpful after gulpful, the water violated his body as the current pulled, twisted, and rolled him. He struggled against it to no avail and had it not been for the slit he had put in his stomach, he surely would have been weighed down by the water he was forced to swallow. The bitter, acrid taste of ash lingered on his tongue and he tried to keep his mouth closed, but the vile water proved relentless. It splashed up into his nasal cavity and dripped into the back of his throat.

At the river's edge he caught sight of movement. He focused and strained to see a pack of the largest wolves he had ever seen. Their mane of brown fur blew wildly behind their heads as they ran along the riverbank, their claws long and bloodstained, hunger burning in their red eyes.

The sound of a whip cracking caused the wolves to disperse, and John's momentum to stop as the whip wrapped around his throat. The wolves quickly regrouped and stood together at the riverbank. As the water rushed by, he was able to turn himself around to see a winged demon knee deep in the water. While stepping back toward land, the demon reeled him in as if he was a fish on a hook. It pulled him ashore, out of the sulfuric water and along the soft, cold earth. When the winged creature finally stopped, he simply lay there in the thick mud, his muscles exhausted from their struggle to keep him afloat.

From the other side of the river, the wolves barked their displeasure at the lost meal.

"Master is expecting you," the demon said, bending over.

Can't let him, he thought as he pushed down into the ground to try and lift himself. His elbows wobbled under his weight and the saturated ground swallowed his hands. *Must fight.*

As the creature drew ever closer, John curled a fist in the black mud and then pulled his hand free. He hurled the blackish goop up into the demon's face, striking it in the eyes.

"Uh!" it bellowed as it took a step back.

The creature's clawed hands shot toward its face to wipe away the mud and John took the opportunity to get to his feet and run. His legs trembled as he pressed forward, threatening him to stumble with each footfall. The soft earth under him added to his fear of falling face-first to the ground.

"Foolish human!"

Don't look back, he told himself.

"There is no escape from me!"

Keep running.

With no bearings on where he was and no clue on how to get out of the pit, he ran. The muscles of his legs tightened and cramped, he forced himself to press on, afraid of the alternative. Out of the darkness before him, two wolves barked and lunged toward him. He tried to stop running, but the ground provided no traction and his feet slipped out from under him. He fell to his backside and slid through the mud. The wolves flew over him and they whimpered. John turned around to see the wolves collapse to the ground. He stared up at the winged devil with unblinking eyes. Blood dripped from its talon-like claws.

"I should have let them feast on your flesh," the creature said, and bent forward and scooped him up into its massive arms.

John had neither the strength nor inclination to resist any further. As they traveled through Hell, he took in all there was to see, knowing full well that one day he'd call this place home. Just outside the river bank they passed under a wrought iron arch with the words: *Lasciate ogne speranza, voi ch'intrate* detailed in the frame work.

"All hope abandon, ye who enter here," the demon spoke in a deep, reverberating voice.

John swallowed hard.

The walls were black with veins of red glowing throughout and lined with iron bars. Atrophied men and women in brown, tattered robes reached through the bars, begging for mercy, as if he had any power to grant it.

They came across a vast expanse of land, home to an orchard of pomegranate trees with workers tending to the soil. There was no mistaking their dense foliage of narrow, oblong leaves, multiple stems, the red and purple fruit.

This is Pluto's garden, he thought, looking straight up at the plateau where the god of the underworld looked over his kingdom.

John narrowed his eyes at the figures as they passed. On closer inspection he saw what he thought were slaves tilling the soil were, in fact, men and women feeding the plants with their blood. The roots of the trees entangled their flesh, sucking the life out of them in what John could only think of as a means to sweeten the tree's fruit. The withered carcass of one of the donors fell to the ground. The demonic guards hoisted the body up by its underarms and dragged it to the nearest cell. The cage door slid open and they tossed the dead man inside. The other slaves inside the cage herded to the back, screaming. The guards snatched another man and pulled him from the crowd while the crowd inside the cage tended to the man they replaced.

The cage closed, and the unfortunate man was thrown before the tree. He screamed as he stood, but thorned vines quickly snaked their way to his legs before he could take a retreating step. The thorns punctured his flesh, and blood flowed once more.

John knew the man who'd fallen would get to rest momentarily. For how long, he could not tell. It was obvious this place was a constant cycle of pain. He couldn't help but wonder if this was to be his eventual fate, or if Pluto had something much worse in mind for him.

CHAPTER TEN

Once atop the plateau, the demon tossed John before the god of the underworld. When John tried to stand, the winged-beast pressed his hoofed foot against his back and pushed him down. When John remained on his knees of his own accord, the demon stepped away.

"Very foolish," said the god, his voice so loud it reverberated inside John's chest. "The flesh of those children was not for your lips."

"I was hungry. And they stumbled upon me."

"You will always be hungry. No food or drink can satiate you. That's part of your penance."

"And what else is my penance? Having to obey the beast that once looked upon me as its master? Isn't that suffering enough? And what about the pain the sun causes me?"

"All a part of your living hell. But keeping you out of the sun is also a benefit to you, for the heat would increase your rate of decay. Besides, it gives you the time you need to think about what you've done. Now . . . this is not why I've summoned you here. Did I not make myself clear that you are to deliver me the wicked?"

John narrowed his eyes at the bulbous god. "You did . . . and I have."

"Yes, but you have also condemned the souls of two innocents."

Pluto waved his hand and bubbling magma seeped up from the floor before John. He leaned back; fearful of it melting his flesh, but it quickly became obvious that was not its intent. Inside the puddle, an image of a woman knelt down beside a running stream appeared. He watched as the two teenagers he had slaughtered stepped out of the woods behind her. She was merely washing clothing, oblivious to their approach.

"Is that—?"

"Eidolons? Yes."

Dangling above the walking corpses were the pale silhouettes of his victims. Much like he had followed the cat around on the day he was hung, their spirits were trapped, connected to their undead bodies by a silver umbilical cord.

"Not destined for Hell, and cursed by your hunger, their souls are trapped in limbo. Forced to watch as their former selves slaughter any who cross their path. And as they rise up, so too will their victims."

"What can I do?"

"There is nothing you can do except for not allowing it to happen again. There is only one I trust to set this right. This calls for the service of my most loyal servant."

Without uttering another word, a black fog rose out of the pit and cascaded across the floor. It gathered in between Pluto and John and took shape. Four powerful paws pressed against the stone, legs took shape, followed by a muscular body, a tail and three heads. John trembled at the sight of the behemoth. Its mane reminded him of Medusa's hair, dozens of serpents jetting from behind its heads—all looking directly at him. Their forked tongues tasted the air before him as if determining whether he was friend or foe. The tail swung over John's head and slammed on the ground to his right. The stone chipped away under its brute strength.

"Cerberus, set them free."

The beast exploded into a plume of black smog and vanished from sight. When John returned his gaze to the puddle of magma, he saw the woman's body being ravaged by his creations. Her eyes stared lifelessly back at him as the two creatures tore into her flesh. Blood and intestine flowed from her open abdomen into the riverbank as they gorged themselves on her body.

Unable to look away, he jealously watched as they feasted and saw the same black fog permeate from the woods. Cerberus formed from the shadows and pounced in between the young couple. The left head snapped its powerful jaws on the girl's skull, the right clamped down on the boy's, and the center just drooled long strands of saliva onto their victim. Blood spilled from the points of impact. Their eyes bulged from their sockets as the pressure mounted, and in the blink of an eye, simultaneously their heads exploded in a crimson rain. Their bodies dropped and convulsed, pumping more blood into the soil, until they finally lay still.

Cerberus's center head sniffed the woman, her hair whipping upward with each breath from its maw. It growled, then stomped on her head. Brain matter jettisoned outward in all directions. Chunky bits of gore clung to the bodies of her attackers and the ground.

"You could learn a thing or two from Cerberus," said Pluto with that devilish grin.

"I'm not your dog," John said, standing.

"So you say. It would behoove you to follow the cat and kill only those it selects for you."

John laughed. "Surely a god in your position would know that I killed the infernal beast."

"Surely a man of your intellect would not be so ignorant to think that he could kill a servant of Pluto's so easily. It will take much more than a broken neck to put it down."

Damn. "I could be persuaded to cooperate with the beast. All I ask is for it to take me to the men who defiled my beloved."

"Still blaming others for your own misguided deeds. Very well. Now, be gone with you, knave."

Pluto waved his hand and the air around John bubbled. His surroundings changed from the plateau to the sepulchre, and Pluto's final words echoed in his ears: "Do not fail me again."

A long, deep growl caused John's head to sink into his shoulders. He turned around to see the cat standing on the stone steps, conveniently surrounded by the sunlight penetrating the crypt. It hissed, baring its teeth. John pursed his lips and curled his hands into fists.

"Smart devil," he said.

Though he had missed it briefly, seeing the cat now reminded him of why he had snapped its neck in the first place. As the two locked gazes, John noticed one of its back legs was no longer black, but now a solid white like its underbelly.

What does it mean? he wondered. *Could it possibly be a signifier, a manifestation of the nine lives a cat is said to have?*

Despite his unwanted connection to the cat, the question went unanswered, but he knew it to be the only logical explanation. Given the sun's reach into the crypt, John determined there was still at least four hours of daylight left. Resting his back against the far wall, he allowed himself to slide down the stone surface until he was in a sitting position. With a sigh, he waited.

Time passed slowly with neither ghoul nor beast making any advancement toward the other. A distrust suffocated the air, and all either of them could do was wait for dusk, and when it finally came, the two set their differences aside and obeyed their master's wishes.

Upon exiting the crypt, John turned to the cat and said, "Take me to one of the . . . charlatans who condemned my Madeline's soul."

The cat stood there and blankly stared at him.

"If her soul is to be condemned, then so shall theirs. With or without your help."

The cat meowed and proceeded to lead the way.

That's more like it, John thought, and followed.

As they traveled through Bigler's Mill, passing by the brightly-painted frame houses and brick houses of the wealthy, John recognized the path they were taking. It was the same route he drunkenly traversed on a regular basis. And when he lifted his head to gaze further down the street to confirm his suspicion, he saw the house he had failed to make a home for him and Madeline. Though the building was a far cry from the estate that had accidentally burned down, it had been all they could afford and had been warmer—cozier—than the jail cell he had called home for six months. It was a frame house—much like some of the wealthier in town—however, the white-wash paint was faded and dingy. But in the poorer region of town, where the houses were made of large timbers and thatch roofs, his humble abode stood out like a beacon.

He continued to follow the cat and saw his neighbors' houses for the first time with sober eyes. The residents here dismissed cleanliness; bones, broken dishes, and even fecal matter littered the houses' perimeters.

Did I really force Madeline to live in such filth? The idea stung like the demon's whip, but its cut ran deeper. *I should have made the most of it. For that, I am sorry, Madeline.*

John quickened his pace after noticing the cat had put some distance between them. Why had the foul creature brought him here? What did it want to show him? Why couldn't it for once do as *he* wished? These questions ran through his mind as he closed the distance, and as he got closer to his home, he noticed its windows broken in; the front door swung at a crooked angle on one hinge; and the bulk head to the cellar was open.

Rageful pride boiled his blood and without thought, he scooped the cat off the ground and into a chokehold. With his hands firmly wrapped around its throat, he shook it. "Why are you torturing me?"

The cat refused to fight back, angering John further. He removed one hand from around the cat's throat, reeled its body back with the other, and tossed the feline. It screeched as its body soared through the air. It struck the back of the house and fell to the ground where it lay wailing in pain, a streak of blood ran down the clapboard.

"Who's out there?" came a strange voice somewhere from the cellar of John's house.

In his approach he failed to notice the bulkhead open.

Who could that be? And what are they doing here? John ducked behind a row of low-lining bushes.

John watched as a man craned his neck out of the bulkhead and into the moonlight. The man checked left, then right and saw the cat.

I recognize that face, he thought as he pictured the two men who scowled at him during the hanging.

"Pluto, is that you?" asked the man as he made his way out of John's cellar. "Where have you been? Are you hurt?" The man scooped the beast up into his arms, stood up straight and peered out into the darkness, surveying the surrounding areas. The man checked his hand and rubbed his fingertips together. "You're bleeding. Who did this to you?" he asked as if the creature could answer. "Come on inside. Maybe there's a blanket or something I can wrap you in."

John waited for the man to disappear from sight before abandoning his hiding spot. He approached the cellar's entrance slowly, mindful of his step so as not to snap a twig and alert the stranger. Once at the bulkhead, he dropped to all fours and craned his neck to see inside the cellar. There, the man stood with the cat in his arms before the hollowed-out wall where John had sealed Madeline away.

"Look who came to visit, Mad," he said.

Mad? John thought. *And they said I was a lunatic. How long was this going on that he had a pet name for her? Worse, how did he even find her?*

The man stroked the cat down its back, up its tail, and then returned his hand to the top of the cat's head before doing it all over again. "You should have been with me instead of that good-for-nothin'. I hope he's rottin' in Hell for what he did to you."

From the looks of the man, John figured Madeline had chosen to stay married to him—to endure the suffering he cast on her—for monetary reasons. Though they had lost most of their fortune to his drinking and the fire, there was still enough to live off of without fear. The man's tattered and soiled pants and shirt couldn't say the same for the stranger, and the lack of a jacket with the cool night chill, John doubted he could provide anything but affection to a woman of Madeline's stature.

How could she soil herself with such a vagabond?

The cellar floor was void of clutter. With the man foolishly keeping his back to the cellar's entrance, John snuck up on him with ease.

Just as his hands were about to close in around the man's neck, the cat hissed and lunged out of the man's grip.

"What the—?" He spun around and went wide-eye at the sight of John. "It's you."

John's hands clasped around the man's throat and he applied all the pressure his dead arms could muster.

"It's not . . . possible . . . you're . . . dead," the man said in between gasps for breath. His hands clamped around John's wrists and he struggled to pry him off.

Up close, under the grime, John had to admit the man was handsome. He could see now how Madeline might have fallen for his deep-blue eyes that despite his rugged features relayed compassion and warmth; and standing at six-foot-two, the shape of his biceps and pectorals were well-defined under his shirt and were neither intimidating or uninviting.

As John felt his grip slip, he leaned in, with his mouth wide, and bit into the right side of the man's face. He pulled back, taking skin and flesh with him, and released his hold. Before the man's hand shot upward to cover his cheek, John saw through the hole he had left, a fleshy window to the man's teeth and tongue.

The man let loose with a deep, pain-ridden scream that would no doubt bring the neighbors running. He probed the wound and the look of shock on his face when his finger poked through the hole in his cheek put a smile on John's own. "What are you?" he asked.

"Death!"

John lunged forward, throwing his weight into the man and tackled him to the floor. Though every fiber of his being wanted to punish him, devour his flesh one bite at a time and drag out his death, he didn't know how much time he had, so he wasted none. Like a wild animal, he tore through the man's throat and allowed the blood to spray his face and the front of his shirt. And as the man took his final breath, John plunged his hand into his abdomen and began pulling out the tubular intestine he had grown so fond of.

The cat sat off to the side grooming itself. Despite the affection it showed the man, it did not protest against John's defiling fury.

As he stood, John gazed into the man's glossed-over eyes, then raked his fingers down the man's face. Strips of skin pulled away from his forehead, nose, and chin. He smiled at the carnage and sucked the flesh out from under his fingernails. "Should you see my Madeline in Hell, I doubt she will find you attractive anymore."

Neither neighbors nor policemen came to investigate the scream. But John's meal had grown cold and lost its appeal. He needed to find another source of food. As if reading his mind, the cat stood and walked toward the cellar steps.

"Are you going to take me to Madeline's other lover?" he asked. "And any others who are responsible for sending her to Hell?"

The cat did not respond; instead, it gracefully climbed the steps and darted ahead.

John followed the cat out of the town and through the outlining woods. They headed in the opposite direction of the corpses of the young couple he had condemned. And though he desperately wanted to go into town and claim his next meal, the cat obviously had other plans. They walked, and continued to walk well beyond the town's limits, wasting precious twilight hours.

"Where are you taking me?" he asked the cat as if it could answer.

It ignored him, not even bothering to give him a sideways glance.

"You can't tell me there are no more wicked souls in Bigler's Mill. What about the other man I suspect of bedding my wife? My revenge is not yet complete."

The cat continued to walk, not missing a step.

"Damn you, beast."

Over the treetops, there was a ribbon of smoke. *Someone's out here*, he thought. Just a few feet ahead of them, a light caught his eye. They stepped into a clearing and found a log cabin.

I wonder who lives there? He looked around and took in the surroundings. It was a humble abode of modest size with few windows, a woodpile lined neatly beside the cabin, a wraparound porch with two rabbits strung from their back legs dangling from a lattice trimming the porch roof.

He walked closer, treading carefully. Fallen leaves and twigs littered the ground and John couldn't take the chance of stepping into a bear trap, which he felt a man in tuned with nature out here all alone would most certainly have. The first porch step creaked as his weight pressed down upon it. He stopped, frozen in anticipation. Whoever was inside was too preoccupied to care or didn't hear the subtle warning of an intruder. Either way, John continued.

Balancing his weight as best he could, he walked around the porch to the first window. The curtains were drawn, but the fabric was thin enough to allow him to see inside to the kitchen area. A small animal was skinned and on the chopping block. He saw no one and continued to the next window. He peered inside the living area and still saw no one.

There's no one here, he thought, and just as he was about to turn back, a flap in the floor boards folded over and a man climbed out. *What's that sound?* He strained his ears to hear a metallic rustling coming from beneath the floor.

"I don't want to hear another peep from you. Understand?" The man slammed the trapdoor shut, silencing the peculiar sound, then walked back to the kitchen.

John did not recognize him, and he couldn't recall ever seeing him in town. He wouldn't have given the trapdoor a second thought had he simply closed the door and carried on his way. But now he knew without a doubt, the man was intended to feed his undying appetite. It was obvious to John that a dark secret was buried beneath those floorboards. He walked back to the front of the cabin and rapped his knuckles against the door.

"Whatever it is, I ain't interested," he heard the man say.

He thumped the door again.

"Go away!"

With a curled fist, he pounded on the door harder.

"I got a gun and I aims to use it."

John stepped to the side of the door and waited, hoping the man's own guilt and anxiety would cause him to make a mistake similar to his own that cost him his freedom. *How could I have been so foolish as to tap the wall where I had sealed Madeline in?* Though he didn't understand the inner workings of the human psyche, John knew he could count on it. The door cracked open and the barrel of a smoothbore musket poked out.

"Who's there? Show yourself," demanded the man from the doorway.

John grabbed the barrel of the gun and pulled the man onto the porch. The gun went off and warmth permeated John's cold flesh.

"Damn, boy, you smell to high Hell." His nose wrinkled in disgust.

Enraged by the indignity of it all, John wrestled the gun from the man, then buried its stock into the center of his face. The nose bent to the left and blood flowed freely down his face and dripped onto the front of his shirt.

"My nose!" The man's hands shot toward his face as he took a step back. "It's broken!"

"That's the least of your concerns," John said, dropping the gun and tackling him to the ground. He clamped his teeth onto the front of the man's neck and ripped out his throat, letting the blood spray upon his face.

The man placed his hands against John's shoulders and tried to push him off, but his strength ebbed too quickly. The elbows bent before the arms fell lifeless to his chest. John stood and inspected his side. The musket had blown a chunk of his dead flesh away from the right side of his waist. Black, tar-like ooze ran down the outside of his pant leg from his putrefying organs.

Time for a new shirt, he thought as he grabbed the body by the ankles and dragged him inside. A streak of blood painted the floor behind him.

"What were you hiding down there?" he asked, not expecting an answer. "Whatever it is, I'm sure it can wait until after I've eaten."

CHAPTER ELEVEN

When John had finished devouring the man's delectable parts, he walked over to the trapdoor in the center of the living area. He stood there, hovering over it as he pondered what mysteries lay in the darkness of the cellar. As he bent at the knees to open the trapdoor, the cat strolled into the room from outside.

"Where've you been? Find a juicy squirrel or plump rat, did you?" John cracked a smile then returned his attention to the door. Though the act of talking cute to the cat sickened him, knowing the god of the underworld was watching them, he felt the need to try and establish a relationship with the beast. Even a parasitic relationship could be built on solid ground.

He flipped the door open and peered into the darkness. A soft whimper echoed from within the room.

Going to need a torchlight first, he thought, looking around the room.

A candle was perched on the fireplace's mantle. He retrieved it and then dipped the wick into the roaring fire. Embers danced outward, falling on his shirt sleeve. "Ooh!" He patted out the tiny flame clinging to his wrist out of instinct, then returned to the trapdoor.

The cat stepped aside as he prepared to descend the small staircase. The stairs wobbled with each shaky step. The tiny flame illuminated the darkness below to reveal a small room. The walls were nothing more than the compacted earth under the house; roots from neighboring trees penetrated the room and hung in the air; and just ahead at the bottom of the stairs, a cage with a young girl of fifteen or sixteen years of age was crammed inside. She was scrunched together on all fours, the cage big enough to house a large wolf or dog. The girl's body trembled as he approached and the cat wailed its disapproval.

He turned to face the beast, which still stood at the top of the stairs. "Fine. She will not suffer my bite."

Turning back to the girl and bringing the candlelight closer to her face, he saw her dilated pupils shrink. Caked-on grime rimmed her eyes; her jawbone was cocked at an odd angle, and the torn rags of her clothing barely clung to her slender frame. Without the young girl uttering a single word, John knew full well what was going on here.

"I'm not going to hurt you," he said in the softest voice his dry, coarse vocal cords could muster.

Tears streamed from her eyes as she pointed to the lock on the door, then to a key ring hanging from a peg in the dirt wall.

"No . . . no . . . I cannot. I'm sorry, my dear. Dawn will soon break and I must spend the daylight hours here. I can ill afford you bringing the authorities back with you. We shall keep each other company until the sun sets, then part ways. I promise."

She tucked her chin into her bosom and looked away from him, heartbreak on her face. Was it her displeasure with him not freeing her, or his own decaying hideousness that made it so she could not look upon him?

"Can you talk?" he asked, but feared she could not. Her jaw hung lower than normal as if it was unhinged.

She tried to speak, but only mumbled incoherently, a series of moans and sobs. Finally, she shook her head side-to-side.

"Are you hungry?" His concern surprised even him. Here he was, a predator, showing sympathy to his prey. *No*, he thought, *she is an innocent. I mustn't.*

She nodded excitedly and John couldn't help but wonder how long the bastard, who lay in a pool of his own blood upstairs, had kept her down here in the dark, away from civilization. *Is she at least educated?* He placed the candle on a stool near the cage so she wouldn't be left alone in the blackness, and then turned back toward the stairs.

"I'll go fix you something to eat. I'll be right back."

Once he was out of the make-shift cellar, the cat trotted down the stairs. He snubbed his nose at the beast as it passed and made his way toward the kitchen, remembering the skinned animal he had seen earlier. On the counter, potatoes and carrots had been peeled and were waiting to be put into a pot.

It would seem I caught him in the middle of making a stew. What an odd time to be fixin' a meal, he thought. *What kind of hours did he keep? Wonder if he was going to share it with his guest?*

He eyed the meat. "BAH!" Swiping his arm across the counter, he knocked it to the floor and set his sights on something more fitting. The man's half-eaten body lay sprawled out, face-down on the floor under the archway between rooms. There was a knife on the counter, which he grabbed, then walked to the body, knowing he could still slice a decent size piece of steak from his thigh and buttocks.

"I think the young lady would want her pound of flesh from you, wouldn't you agree?" he said playfully as he stabbed the knife's blade into the right cheek.

He carved a hunk of meat out of the carcass and carried it to the kitchen where he skinned and cubed the meat before tossing it in a pot along with the potatoes and carrots. After filling the pot halfway with water, he returned to the living area and hung the pot over the fire.

"There we are," he said. "Should be ready in a bit."

While the stew boiled, John searched the man's wardrobe for a suitable shirt. Undressed, he caught sight of the blackened flesh in a mirror attached to the dresser and a blackish stain covering his buttocks on his once beige pants. *My organs are liquefying and seeping out,* he thought, and then grabbed a fresh pair of slacks from the closet as well. *How much longer is my body going to last?* Realizing it was out of his hands, he washed and dressed, then returned to the fireplace and sat down to wait.

When he felt it was ready, he ladled out a plate and brought it downstairs to the young woman. Without knowing how long it had been since her last meal, he didn't give her too much, fearful of her stuffing herself and making her sick. He knew it was cruel to keep her locked in the cage, and she needed medical attention, but he had no choice. His own survival dictated his actions.

"Here you go, my dear," he said, sliding the plate through the opening in the cage under its door.

She took the plate and shoveled the food into her mouth with her bare hands as he had expected. He smiled as she trustingly devoured the food he presented her with. The thought of telling her she was eating the flesh of her tormentor crossed his mind, but he decided she had been through enough. He wondered if this simple act of kindness would show him mercy when he finally entered Hell permanently, but he somehow doubted it.

If serving Pluto does not grant me pass from the tortures of Hell, then helping one insignificant girl won't either.

He sat there in the dark, cramped space with the girl. Her whimpers as she slept broke the silence briefly, and when she was awake, he didn't know what to say to her. He could list out all the terrible possibilities of her abuse, the atrocities he would commit to such a lovely thing, and see just how similar he was to the monster upstairs, but what purpose would it serve him other than delight his twisted mind? Certainly it would only pain the girl further, and from the looks of her bruised and battered body, her suffering would continue well after the cage door was opened and she was finally set free.

Through the bars, she stroked the cat's black and white fur. Even after the horrors she was forced to endure, she still had a gentle heart and it sickened John. It was a testament to her strength and his lack thereof. Growing up, he had had a good life: far better than most, yet he was never satisfied. He witnessed the suffering of others and reveled in it. From the torn clothing some of his classmates had to wear during the winter months, to the beggars on the street, misery was all around him, but never his own. His belly always full and his bed warm, yet something inside him was different. What was it that made him delight in the suffering of others? He would never know.

Movement in his arm distracted his mind and he held up the appendage to the light. Under the flaps of skin caused by the cat's claws, maggots writhed in his dead flesh.

It was a mistake to hide here, he thought, realizing this was nothing more than an open grave. He plucked a white larva from his forearm and stared at it. His stomach ached and longed for what he could not have. *Maybe...* He tossed the insect into his mouth and bit down. There was a faint trace of flesh in its flavor and he quickly tugged another one out. One by one, he plucked the plump parasites out of his flesh and mashed them between his teeth. But they were not enough to appease his hunger.

When the sun finally set, he opened the cage door and escorted the girl up the stairs. Upon seeing the man who had tortured her lying dead and mangled on the floor, she smiled a twisted grin.

Good for you, he thought as they walked past. The cat was already outside sitting in the direction John thought it wanted them to travel.

I wonder which direction would be more suitable for her? Knowing it was safer for her to travel with them to the next town, he guided her toward the cat. The cat stood abruptly. The hairs along its back went rigid as it hissed. The girl stopped, obviously frightened by the outburst and looking confused after it had been so nice to her earlier.

She can't come. "All right, if you keep walking in that direction," he said, pointing to his left, "you'll come to Bigler's Mill. You should find an officer walking the beat. They'll help you."

The girl looked at him with wide eyes and trembling lips. For the first time she saw him for what he truly was, the undead, without the concealment of shadows and yet, her first instinct was not to run away. Though John found it curious, he could not deny the power of gratitude. *Perhaps her interpretation of what a monster truly is has been altered?*

"No need to be afraid. Nothing's going to hurt you."

She grabbed his hand and pulled.

"I can't go with you," he said.

With both hands on his, she pulled again, a low grunt emanating from her as she did.

"No!" He pulled back, freeing his hand. "I can't go back there. Please understand."

Tears filled her eyes and if his heart was alive he knew it would have ached. She looked so hurt, so pathetic. She turned away from him and ran in the direction he had pointed in.

"Happy?" He snarled at the cat. "I don't see the harm in letting her come with us."

The cat turned away and carried on.

Wretched beast. You won't let me eat her, and you won't let me help her. He grunted, then gritted his teeth. With a shrug, he followed, wondering where they were heading. *Williamsburg is a possibility or perhaps a small settlement such as Magruder. Yes, that would seem to be the most likely candidate. They have their own cemetery behind the church with a few homes outlining the town.*

A scream broke the silence.

The girl!

John turned around and ran back the way he came. He passed by the log cabin and back into the woods. A horrid mixture of snarls and slurps echoed in the air.

No.

The girl lay face down in the dirt before him. Two wolves turned toward him. As one, they released a low, guttural growl at the interruption of their meal. Their muzzles stained in blood, heads low to the ground, they locked their eyes onto him, the hair on the back of their necks standing up straight.

"Git!"

The wolves barked and snapped their jaws; his final warning he knew, but something inside kept him rooted to the spot. Whether it was an instinctual need to fight over a potential meal or the possibility he actually cared for another human being he did not know. One thing was sure: he was not going to allow these scavengers to have her.

He stepped forward and one of the wolves lunged. He caught the animal in midair around the throat, twirled his body round, and slammed the beast's spine against a nearby oak tree. The wolf bellowed in pain as it fell to the ground.

With him distracted, its partner managed to sink its teeth into his forearm. It growled as it pulled against him in an effort to rip the limb from his torso. He slammed his fist into the wolf's face, right between the eyes. It whimpered as it released its bite. Before it could run away, John grabbed it by the jaws and applied pressure. He forced the jaws apart until they snapped and the wolf fell at his feet.

He turned back to the other wolf. Its hind legs thrashed as it tried to stand, but its broken back was evident. John walked over to the beast, knelt down and picked up a rock, then smashed its skull in. When the beast finally stopped flailing, he dropped the rock and walked over to the girl. He saw her bottom jaw on the ground a foot away. He steeled his nerves.

This isn't going to be pretty, he thought as he gently rolled her over. She looked at him with tear-filled eyes and he could see his guilt reflected in them. Her tongue wildly flopped to the rhythmic gurgling sounds of blood dripping down the back of her throat. The girl was strong, there was no denying that, but the damage was irreversible.

"I'm sorry," he said.

She reached out and touched his hand. The gesture was a warm welcome. He felt the sting of guilt for not even knowing her name.

"You still have so much life, don't you?"

She looked at him with longing and nodded.

What do I do? If I bite her, I'll stop her suffering but condemn her soul in the process.

The cat meowed as it approached.

"This is your fault. Your fault!" He pulled away from the girl and snatched the cat by the back of the head and lifted it up to look it in the eye.

The cat extended its claws and raked them across the side of his face. He squeezed and applied enough pressure to cause the cat's eye to bulge outward in its socket. In an effort to break its back, he shook it violently.

"Wretched beast, haunt me no longer!"

He slammed its head against a nearby rock and leaned all his weight into it. A trickle of blood ran down the rock's surface as he maintained pressure. The cat screamed as its flesh and bone collapsed under John's weight. Blood and chunks of pinkish-gray brain matter clung to his hand as he lifted it off the rock face.

"Ach!" With the flick of his wrist, the gore flung away.

The young girl tried to sit up, but he quickly extended his arm out to stop her. Once at her side, with one hand at her back, and one taking her hand in his, he guided her back to the ground. "What can I do?"

She tried to speak, but was unable to form the words.

Her eyes say it all, he thought. The idea of caving in her skull with a rock crossed his mind, but it felt too violent, likewise strangling her. With no other options, he cradled her head against his chest and looked to the heavens.

"O Heavenly Father, though I have no right to beseech a favor of You for my soul is tainted, I do so not for my benefit, but for this lost soul. I know she is destined to sit at Your side, to bask in Your glory. Please, I beg You, end her suffering. Take her in Your loving embrace and comfort her as I cannot."

John returned his gaze to the young girl. She choked back blood as her pupils narrowed. He felt the strength in her hand ebb and knew this was it, her dying breaths. If his dead eyes could muster an ounce of moisture, tears would surely flow from even his cold, dark heart. He watched over her, held her hand tight as her body convulsed before finally drifting away into the afterlife.

"Goodbye," he said as he closed her eyelids with his fingers.

Without a hiss or a screech, John felt the claws of the cat dig into the dead flesh of his shoulder, its teeth sinking into his neck. He reached round and grabbed hold of the beast by the midsection and pulled it off him, taking a considerable chunk of flesh with him. The cat screamed and clawed and John noticed both rear legs now solid white.

By his count, the cat still had five lives left before it would stay dead.

At least, he hoped it would.

Hungry, and unwilling to eat the flesh of the young girl before it lost its heat, he opened his mouth wide and clamped down on the back of the cat's neck. It roared in pain as he ripped it apart, bite by bite. Not bothering to chew, he just swallowed flesh and fur in rapid succession. He broke the bones into tiny, bite size pieces and tossed them into his gullet and didn't stop until the beast was completely in his bulbous stomach.

"It's a shame my body no longer defecates," he said, thinking it to be the ultimate revenge.

When he stood, a fire burned in his belly warming him from the inside out. A paw protruded from the self-inflicted wound, turned upward and was dragged through his flesh toward his chin. His hands shot toward the opening in hopes of keeping the beast inside him, but the cat emerged with such force, he was knocked back and fell to the ground. The cat pounced onto his chest, looked him dead in the eye, and then breathed in deeply. John watched, wide-eyed, as the blue fog with pulsating veins of white passed over his lips and back into the cat's mouth. The white fur of its back legs turned black as the cat reclaimed the life it had sacrificed for him. Darkness crept over his vision from the corners of his eyes until the world faded away.

***

"I had high hopes for you, John. Shame you couldn't keep your emotions in check. Alas..."

Pluto took his eyes off his newest servant and gazed at the large, purplish-skinned pomegranate. The delectable fruit was perfect in color and size, his pudgy hand barely able to hold it. Wondering if it tasted as sweet as it appeared to, he brought it to his full lips and sank his teeth in. Nectar filled his mouth as the seeds inside were squashed. His tongue rolled across his lips. Pieces of fruit clung to the fleshy muscle, and as his tongue passed Pluto's front teeth the half-eaten pieces fell away.

He held the fruit up at an angle and smiled. "Delicious."

A seed fell from the fruit's core and bounced off his gelatinous belly only to slide down and disappear into one of the many rolls of skin. He looked down at the sticky trail, then toward his servant.

"Slave, you missed a spot."

With no free will, John Mohr dipped his sponge in the bucket of water, separated the folds of skin with his free hand, and washed his master.

THE TELL-TALE HEART
by Edgar Allan Poe

TRUE!—nervous—very, very dreadfully nervous I had been and am; but why will you say that I am mad? The disease had sharpened my senses—not destroyed—not dulled them. Above all was the sense of hearing acute. I heard all things in the heaven and in the earth. I heard many things in hell. How, then, am I mad? Hearken! and observe how healthily—how calmly I can tell you the whole story.

It is impossible to say how first the idea entered my brain; but once conceived, it haunted me day and night. Object there was none. Passion there was none. I loved the old man. He had never wronged me. He had never given me insult. For his gold I had no desire. I think it was his eye! yes, it was this! He had the eye of a vulture—a pale blue eye, with a film over it. Whenever it fell upon me, my blood ran cold; and so by degrees—very gradually—I made up my mind to take the life of the old man, and thus rid myself of the eye forever.

Now this is the point. You fancy me mad. Madmen know nothing. But you should have seen me. You should have seen how wisely I proceeded—with what caution—with what foresight—with what dissimulation I went to work! I was never kinder to the old man than during the whole week before I killed him. And every night, about midnight, I turned the latch of his door and opened it—oh so gently! And then, when I had made an opening sufficient for my head, I put in a dark lantern, all closed, closed, that no light shone out, and then I thrust in my head. Oh, you would have laughed to see how cunningly I thrust it in! I moved it slowly—very, very slowly, so that I might not disturb the old man's sleep. It took me an hour to place my whole head within the opening so far that I could see him as he lay upon his bed. Ha! would a madman have been so wise as this, And then, when my head was well in the room, I undid the lantern cautiously—oh, so cautiously—cautiously (for the hinges creaked)—I undid it just so much that a single thin ray fell upon the vulture eye. And this I did for seven long nights—every night just at midnight—but I found the eye always closed; and so it was impossible to do the work; for it was not the old man who vexed me, but his Evil Eye. And every morning, when the day broke, I went boldly into the chamber, and spoke courageously to him, calling him by name in a hearty tone, and inquiring how he has passed the night. So you see he would have been a very profound old man, indeed, to suspect that every night, just at twelve, I looked in upon him while he slept.

Upon the eighth night I was more than usually cautious in opening the door. A watch's minute hand moves more quickly than did mine. Never before that night had I felt the extent of my own powers—of my sagacity. I could scarcely contain my feelings of triumph. To think that there I was, opening the door, little by little, and he not even to dream of my secret deeds or thoughts. I fairly chuckled at the idea; and perhaps he heard me; for he moved on the bed suddenly, as if startled. Now you may think that I drew back—but no. His room was as black as pitch with the thick darkness, (for the shutters were close fastened, through fear of robbers,) and so I knew that he could not see the opening of the door, and I kept pushing it on steadily, steadily.

I had my head in, and was about to open the lantern, when my thumb slipped upon the tin fastening, and the old man sprang up in bed, crying out—"Who's there?"

I kept quite still and said nothing. For a whole hour I did not move a muscle, and in the meantime I did not hear him lie down. He was still sitting up in the bed listening;—just as I have done, night after night, hearkening to the death watches in the wall.

Presently I heard a slight groan, and I knew it was the groan of mortal terror. It was not a groan of pain or of grief—oh, no!—it was the low stifled sound that arises from the bottom of the soul when overcharged with awe. I knew the sound well. Many a night, just at midnight, when all the world slept, it has welled up from my own bosom, deepening, with its dreadful echo, the terrors that distracted me. I say I knew it well. I knew what the old man felt, and pitied him, although I chuckled at heart. I knew that he had been lying awake ever since the first slight noise, when he had turned in the bed. His fears had been ever since growing upon him. He had been trying to fancy them causeless, but could not. He had been saying to himself—"It is nothing but the wind in the chimney—it is only a mouse crossing the floor," or "It is merely a cricket which has made a single chirp." Yes, he had been trying to comfort himself with these suppositions: but he had found all in vain. All in vain; because Death, in approaching him had stalked with his black shadow before him, and enveloped the victim. And it was the mournful influence of the unperceived shadow that caused him to feel—although he neither saw nor heard—to feel the presence of my head within the room.

When I had waited a long time, very patiently, without hearing him lie down, I resolved to open a little—a very, very little crevice in the lantern. So I opened it—you cannot imagine how stealthily, stealthily—until, at length a simple dim ray, like the thread of the spider, shot from out the crevice and fell full upon the vulture eye.

It was open—wide, wide open—and I grew furious as I gazed upon it. I saw it with perfect distinctness—all a dull blue, with a hideous veil over it that chilled the very marrow in my bones; but I could see nothing else of the old man's face or person: for I had directed the ray as if by instinct, precisely upon the damned spot.

And have I not told you that what you mistake for madness is but over-acuteness of the sense?—now, I say, there came to my ears a low, dull, quick sound, such as a watch makes when enveloped in cotton. I knew that sound well, too. It was the beating of the old man's heart. It increased my fury, as the beating of a drum stimulates the soldier into courage.

But even yet I refrained and kept still. I scarcely breathed. I held the lantern motionless. I tried how steadily I could maintain the ray upon the eve. Meantime the hellish tattoo of the heart increased. It grew quicker and quicker, and louder and louder every instant. The old man's terror must have been extreme! It grew louder, I say, louder every moment!—do you mark me well I have told you that I am nervous: so I am. And now at the dead hour of the night, amid the dreadful silence of that old house, so strange a noise as this excited me to uncontrollable terror. Yet, for some minutes longer I refrained and stood still. But the beating grew louder, louder! I thought the heart must burst. And now a new anxiety seized me—the sound would be heard by a neighbour! The old man's hour had come! With a loud yell, I threw open the lantern and leaped into the room. He shrieked once—once only. In an instant I dragged him to the floor, and pulled the heavy bed over him. I then smiled gaily, to find the deed so far done. But, for many minutes, the heart beat on with a muffled sound. This, however, did not vex me; it would not be heard through the wall. At length it ceased. The old man was dead. I removed the bed and examined the corpse. Yes, he was stone, stone dead. I placed my hand upon the heart and held it there many minutes. There was no pulsation. He was stone dead. His eye would trouble me no more.

If still you think me mad, you will think so no longer when I describe the wise precautions I took for the concealment of the body. The night waned, and I worked hastily, but in silence. First of all I dismembered the corpse. I cut off the head and the arms and the legs.

I then took up three planks from the flooring of the chamber, and deposited all between the scantlings. I then replaced the boards so cleverly, so cunningly, that no human eye—not even his—could have detected anything wrong. There was nothing to wash out—no stain of any kind—no blood-spot whatever. I had been too wary for that. A tub had caught all—ha! ha!

When I had made an end of these labors, it was four o'clock—still dark as midnight. As the bell sounded the hour, there came a knocking at the street door. I went down to open it with a light heart,—for what had I now to fear? There entered three men, who introduced themselves, with perfect suavity, as officers of the police. A shriek had been heard by a neighbour during the night; suspicion of foul play had been aroused; information had been lodged at the police office, and they (the officers) had been deputed to search the premises.

I smiled, for what had I to fear? I bade the gentlemen welcome. The shriek, I said, was my own in a dream. The old man, I mentioned, was absent in the country. I took my visitors all over the house. I bade them search—search well. I led them, at length, to his chamber. I showed them his treasures, secure, undisturbed. In the enthusiasm of my confidence, I brought chairs into the room, and desired them here to rest from their fatigues, while I myself, in the wild audacity of my perfect triumph, placed my own seat upon the very spot beneath which reposed the corpse of the victim.

The officers were satisfied. My manner had convinced them. I was singularly at ease. They sat, and while I answered cheerily, they chatted of familiar things. But, ere long, I felt myself getting pale and wished them gone. My head ached, and I fancied a ringing in my ears: but still they sat and still chatted. The ringing became more distinct: It continued and became more distinct: I talked more freely to get rid of the feeling: but it continued and gained definiteness—until, at length, I found that the noise was not within my ears.

No doubt I now grew very pale; but I talked more fluently, and with a heightened voice. Yet the sound increased—and what could I do? It was a low, dull, quick sound—much such a sound as a watch makes when enveloped in cotton. I gasped for breath—and yet the officers heard it not. I talked more quickly—more vehemently; but the noise steadily increased. I arose and argued about trifles, in a high key and with violent gesticulations; but the noise steadily increased. Why would they not be gone? I paced the floor to and fro with heavy strides, as if excited to fury by the observations of the men— but the noise steadily increased. Oh God! what could I do? I foamed—I raved—I swore! I swung the chair upon which I had been sitting, and grated it upon the boards, but the noise arose over all and continually increased. It grew louder—

louder—louder! And still the men chatted pleasantly, and smiled. Was it possible they heard not? Almighty God!—no, no! They heard!—they suspected!—they knew!—they were making a mockery of my horror!—this I thought, and this I think. But anything was better than this agony! Anything was more tolerable than this derision! I could bear those hypocritical smiles no longer! I felt that I must scream or die! and now—again!—hark! louder! louder! louder! louder!

"Villains!" I shrieked, "dissemble no more! I admit the deed!—tear up the planks! here, here!—It is the beating of his hideous heart!"

BROKEN
by Keith Gouveia

You may think I'm a sociopath.

You may even sympathize with me.

The fact of the matter is, I don't care what you think of me. I was cheated. Plain and simple. I am merely adapting. There is no spite or malice in what I do.

Not too long ago, I was weak. A quivering mass of flesh walking aimlessly with blinders on, not wanting to see the truth. Last night, my eyes began to open as I came home from a hard day at work.

"Honey, I'm home," I called, entering our Floridian home. Closing the door behind me, I locked it and listened for a response. "Dawn, are you home?" I asked when none came.

Walking through the foyer and into the kitchen, I expected to see my beloved wife preparing dinner. When I found the room empty, I changed course to our bedroom.

Flipping the light on, I found no sign of her, but the bathroom door was closed.

"Oh, thank God," I exclaimed, then walking over to the door I rapped my knuckles on it. "Honey, are you in there? I'm home. What's for dinner, baby?"

Silence.

A myriad of images flashed before my eyes. An image of her naked body sprawled across the floor lying in a puddle of blood from tripping in the shower. Another image of her lifeless body resting against the end of the tub staring at me with her wrists slit, the water crimson red.

No. I shook the images away. My Dawn would never commit suicide. She loved life. Loved me.

"Dawn? Honey, this isn't funny. I'm coming in," I said, grabbing the knob. Thankfully, it was unlocked.

I opened the door and the truth slammed me in the gut as if it was a steam train.

Inside the master bath, I found nothing but darkness.

"Dawn!" I called, then the realization hit me.

Tears pooled in my eyes as the painful memory returned.

The phone call I received two nights ago.

The officer informing me of a tragic accident.

A semi-truck tipping over in the middle of a thunderstorm and landing on top of a car, crushing it.

Dawn's car.

The officer asked me to come and identify the body, but his voice seemed so distant.

No, Dawn was okay, I remembered praying.

It was a mistake.

Had to be a mistake.

But it wasn't.

There she was, lying on a cold slab the mortician pulled out of a wall, wearing nothing but a white sheet. Her neck was no longer defined, just rolled-up flesh. The impact cracked her skull and shattered the vertebrae in her neck, causing her head to scrunch into her shoulders.

Blood.

There was so much blood.

In the darkness, I fell to my knees as my wobbling legs gave out under the weight of my despair.

I wept into my hands, feeling like a lost child. For the first time in nearly fifteen years, I was alone.

My mind refused to accept her death.

For the past two days I had gone to work as scheduled, ignoring the looks and kind words of encouragement from my peers. I blocked it all out and lived happily with my memories prior to the accident that raped me of all I held dear. My thoughts were convoluted and I was disjointed from the world.

After crying for almost an hour, just as I had the night before, I returned to the kitchen. Opening the freezer door, I grabbed the unopened bottle of vodka, unscrewed the top, and planted my weary body on the couch.

Loosening my tie, I took a long chug from the bottle's neck, then grabbed the remote control. I helped myself to another mouthful of the deadly vice before surfing through the channels.

Nothing was on.

Nothing that would numb my mind from the pain.

The pain of my loss.

I took another swig.

Calling someone sounded like a good idea. Perhaps call one of the guys and maybe go out and shoot some pool at our favorite watering hole. That might help take my mind off it—off her.

Nah! I decided against it.

Taking another swig, I glanced at the answering machine. It blinked the number eleven in repeated succession. Instead of pressing the play button, I chugged more of the clear, delectable liquid that brought me closer to freedom, and turned away.

Freedom from the pain, that's what I desired. Freedom from the cursed memories that showed me how good I had it. How lucky I was to have a beautiful woman such as Dawn who returned my love, who accepted all my little idiocies, supported my hobbies, and lovingly took care of me.

She was one in a million.

Irreplaceable.

I didn't want to love another woman. I still don't. I'm thirty-four years old and have loved the same woman for sixteen years. Her memory is ingrained into every ounce of my being. What was life like before her?

Hell.

It's too late to start over.

I just wanted it the way it was, but that was impossible. I knew that much at the time. Staring at the bottom of the bottle as the last of the vodka coursed down my throat, I decided I could no longer go on. I needed to be with Dawn one way or another.

Smashing the bottle against the end table, I raised the jagged glass to my left arm, my crisp, white shirt sleeve protecting my flesh from these despicable desires.

Clinching the neck of the shattered bottle between my front teeth, I rolled up the sleeve. My vision began to blur and I saw multiple arms before me.

Shaking my head, I removed the bottle from my mouth's grip and shakily brought it to my skin.

I slashed at the appendage, but missed.

Closing one eye, I slashed again.

This time, I barely grazed the skin. A small trickle of blood ran down my forearm and dripped off my elbow.

I pushed the pain aside with ease.

The room began to spin as I desperately tried to focus on slicing the pulsating vein that called to me for release, begging to be sliced open and bled dry.

Who was I to deny what my body wanted?

As I raised the make-shift weapon to deliver a fatal blow, my eyes rolled upward. The glass slipped from my grip and shattered into tiny pieces on the tile floor behind the couch. My arm limply fell to the side, and darkness claimed me.

***

Fifteen hours later, I awoke in a pool of sweat.

My white shirt and beige slacks stuck to my dampened flesh. My mouth was parched; my stomach growled. Head throbbing in the aftermath of my liquid dinner, I wondered if this was Hell.

The VCR's LCD screen flashed nine o'clock, telling me I needed to get my ass in gear and get dressed. Dawn's funeral was today in less than two hours.

Trying to stand to my feet, I failed and fell backward. The soft cushions eased my fall, but still my pride was bruised.

"Why did I do this to myself?" I asked, trying to stand again. Before I did, I secured my left hand against the arm of the couch for support.

I still stumbled a bit as I took my first step toward the bedroom, but I didn't fall down. Thank God, because I might have cracked my head open on the unforgiving tile floor.

"Crap!" I said, feeling a warm trickle down my leg. "That's just great."

Stripping the sweaty shirt and piss-stained slacks off, I continued to walk toward the bathroom, and then stepped straight into the shower.

The shower head burst to life as I turned the handle.

The rush of cold water helped me snap back to the reality I desperately tried to run away from. Cupping my hands under the running water, I waited until there was a good amount pooled within my palms then raised them to my mouth. Swishing the water around my dry mouth, I spit it out and watched it flow down the drain, just like my life.

After spending nearly a half hour under the water, I finally toweled off. I wrapped the towel around my waist and walked over to the mirror, taking a hard, long look at the shell I had become.

My eyes were bloodshot and puffy due to the excessive crying, and dark patches resided under them. My shoulder-length brown hair was unkempt and stringy.

The reflection sickened me.

My upper lip curled in disgust as I reached for the brush resting on the marble countertop. I started with the bangs, brushing them aside, and worked my way toward the back.

After securing my hair in a ponytail, I dabbed some deodorant on and exited the room.

I searched the closet for my black suit.

You see, black is a sign of hopelessness. A perfect fit for my mood.

Once dressed, I tossed back a stiff drink then locked the house up, got into the car, and drove to St. Joseph's Church where the ceremony was to take place.

I went through the motions as the shambling, decaying zombies would in those B-horror movies I so loved before my life became one. I don't know how I didn't spot her face in the crowd, but she slipped by me up until I walked onto the cemetery plot. There she was, standing beside the open grave.

"Dawn?" I saw the sun's life giving rays radiating off that angelic face. "Dawn, you came back to me," I shouted with childish glee as I ran to her with open arms.

There was a look of puzzlement upon her face, but I paid no attention as I wrapped my arms around her and squeezed tightly, believing God had answered my prayers and delivered me Heaven on Earth.

That moment was bliss.

"I missed you … oh how I've missed you," I said, squeezing even more tightly.

"Steve … I'm not Dawn … I'm her sister."

Those words struck hard.

I pulled back from her and stared at her.

Shaking my head, I thought, *No. This is Dawn.*

There was no mistaking those rosy cheeks and dimples. Those hazel eyes, those long, exuberant brown hairs blowing in the wind.

My mind still in an alcoholic fog. Then I remembered.

Twins.

"Dawn has a twin sister, Mary," I said, my voice a quiet whisper.

"That's right," she said softly.

I stared at her wide-eyed and released my grip on her arms. She tried to speak to me, but her words fell on deaf ears. All I saw were those luscious lips moving up and down, those same luscious lips that brought me a lifetime of pleasure in a single, unadulterated moment.

"I'm sorry," I said. "I'm so sorry."

I ran away crying even though she shouted for me to come back. I ran straight to the car and left, never looking back, but most importantly, without saying goodbye to the woman I love.

***

How long had I sat in the darkness, secluded from the modern world, content with dwelling in the shadows of yesterday?

I didn't know, nor did I care.

Pain was my only comfort now. The only feeling left in this broken body. I am nothing without Dawn. I couldn't even kill myself. What a loser.

Then the doorbell rang.

"Leave me alone!" I shouted.

It rang again.

"Let me die in peace. Just let me die!"

Another ring. This one longer.

"Gah!" I said, rising to my feet.

I unlocked the door and opened it. "What is . . . ?" my voice trailed off as Mary stood before me, quivering in the rain.

"Can I come in?" she asked.

"Ye-Yes." I stepped to the side, allowing her passage.

"Jeff doesn't know I'm here. He'd probably kill me if he knew after the scene at the cemetery this morning."

"I'm sorry about that," I replied, closing the door behind her. A small smile formed on my face as the vacant

131

look upon Jeff's face that morning flashed inside my mind's eye.

"It's okay. I can only imagine how difficult this is for you. Have you been sitting in the dark? May I turn on a light?"

Without replying, I stretched out my arm and reached for the wall. "Is that better?" I asked after switching the light.

"Yes. Thank you."

"Would you care for something to drink?"

My demeanor was changing for the better and I could feel the creeping darkness that was consuming me retreating into the shadows as hope began to warm my heart.

"Sure. Do you have anything diet?" she said.

"Of course," I replied and trotted off to oblige my guest.

An awkward silence blanketed the house as I poured her a glass of soda.

"Why aren't you taking any time out of work?" she finally asked.

"How do you know that?" I exited the kitchen.

"I asked around."

"Why?"

My smile faded away as I handed her the glass of soda.

"I'm worried about you, that's all. We've been family for twelve years."

"Thirteen," I tersely corrected.

She took a moment, running the numbers. "Yes, you're right. More the reason why I care about you."

Something within me snapped. A tidal wave of emotions crashed upon me and all I could do was struggle to stay afloat. I couldn't hold my tongue.

"Don't you understand that you are just a reminder? Do you understand how much my body craves to grab you and pull you close? How difficult it is for me to look upon the face of the woman I love and not see the love and devotion for me in those beautiful eyes."

Mary stood there mouth gaping after hearing my words.

I took a step toward her. "I know every inch of that slender body. Every curve. Every minor imperfection. I wonder if I can excite you by pushing the same buttons that excited Dawn."

"Steve, that's enough," Mary said, stepping back.

"I used to make her scream with wild passion."

"Steve— "

"I can do the same for you."

A slap across the face was the only thing that stopped my advance.

I just stared at her while rubbing my left cheek.

Without saying another word, Mary placed the glass down and walked to the door and left.

Once again, the house was filled with eerie silence.

I turned my head and peered into the shadows. The one light, barely lighting up the foyer and family room created a host of unpleasant images. Wrapping my arms around myself, the darkness returned and a tear streaked down my cheek.

The conversation replayed in my mind, showing me how much of an ass I was. What a fool. As the conversation continued to unravel, I loathed myself even more, driving me further into the shadows and warping my thoughts into something vile. What have I done? How could I? I saw and heard myself doing it, but couldn't stop. Just couldn't . . .

Then, that heavenly voice soothed me. Rescued me.

It doesn't have to be this way.

"Dawn?" I asked, hearing her sensual voice.

You don't have to be alone anymore.

"I don't?"

She could learn to love you. It could be as it was.

"Yes. But what about Jeff? He'll stand in the way."

Then kill 'im.

"How?"

Oh, I'm sure you can think of something.

And I did.

***

I stood outside Mary and Jeff's bedroom window watching them make love. I found the sight intoxicating. Never could I have imagined how good something so dirty could feel. Though I was anxious to reclaim my beloved, I waited there in the darkness.

After the three-day stint in the shadows, what was a few more hours?

Breaking in would be easy. I had a key. A key that was willingly given to me and my beloved wife.

Once I felt they were soundly sleeping, I made my move.

I opened the door oh so slowly so as not to arouse them. I had been inside the house countless times and knew every inch of it. Walking through the house in the black of night, I entered the bedroom undetected.

Approaching the bed, where Jeff rested peacefully, I raised my ice pick level with Jeff's head.

My right elbow cocked back in preparation, and with all my might, I drove the long, pointed shaft into his left ear, shoving it deep into his cranium, trying my best to keep it level.

Upon impact, Jeff's eyes burst open, his body stiffened, and a gasp of air escaped his lips.

The pointy end of my ten-inch pick exited out his right ear with a tiny chunk of brain matter dangling from its tip. A small trickle of blood ran down the side of his face and splashed onto his pillow. Finally, his body relaxed as his life slipped away.

Mary remained asleep, undisturbed by the death of her husband.

I yanked back, removing the blood-stained weapon, and then walked around the foot of the bed. There, my angel slept.

She looked so peaceful.

I didn't have the heart to wake her.

So now I'm sitting here in the quiet darkness, waiting. I am not alone anymore, and tomorrow . . . in the morning, when she freely awakes, she will be mine.

I will have it the way it was.

Just wait and see.

ABOUT THE AUTHOR

Edgar Allan Poe (January 19, 1809 – October 7, 1849) was an American author, poet, editor, and literary critic, considered part of the American Romantic Movement. Best known for his tales of mystery and the macabre, Poe was one of the earliest American practitioners of the short story, and is generally considered the inventor of the detective fiction genre. He was the first well-known American writer to try to earn a living through writing alone, resulting in a financially difficult life and career.

Poe died in Baltimore at age 40; the cause of his death is unknown and has been variously attributed to alcohol poisoning, brain congestion, cholera, heart disease, and rabies.

ABOUT THE AUTHOR

Keith Gouveia is an accomplished horror and dark fantasy writer and fierce advocate of independent and artisanal publishers. His other recent releases are *Animal Behavior and Other Tales of Lycanthropy, The Goblin Princess* and *The Dead Speak in Riddles.* He is also editor of the horror anthologies, *Bits of the Dead, Skeletal Remains,* and *The Snuff Syndicate.* Keith was born and raised in Fall River, MA, but now lives in Orlando, Florida.

You can keep up to date with all of Keith's projects by friending him on Facebook.

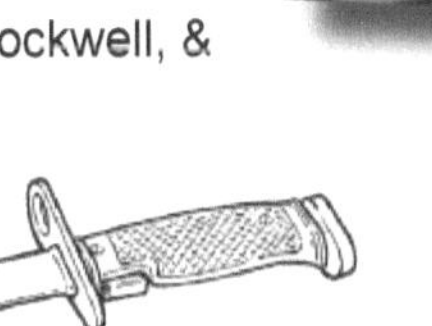

The Snuff Syndicate

In a world where serial killers are usually isolated and disconnected, The Snuff Syndicate provides an online forum where they can brag, ask for advice and revel in their most gratifying hobby.

This anthology includes a novella by Keith Gouveia interwoven with Stories by C.A. Burns, Kevin Cockle, Lorne Dixon, Giovanna Lagana, Mark Onspaugh, Gerald S. Parker, Marsheila Rockwell, & J. T. Seate

Available wherever books are sold!
E-book available at:
Amazon.com, BarnesAndNoble.com, and SmashWords.com

www.ingramcontent.com/pod-product-compliance
Lightning Source LLC
Chambersburg PA
CBHW061453210726
48287CB00007B/2485